The Pushcart War

By Jean Merrill

WITH ILLUSTRATIONS BY

Ronni Solbert

■ HarperCollins*Publishers*

First published by Addison-Wesley Publishing Company

The Pushcart War
Text copyright © 1964 by Jean Merrill
Illustrations copyright © 1964 by Ronni Solbert

Library of Congress Cataloging-in-Publication Data
Merrill, Jean.
    The pushcart war.

    Summary: The outbreak of a war between truck drivers
and pushcart peddlers brings the mounting problems of
traffic to the attention of both the city of New York
and the world.
    1. Children's stories, American. [1. Trucks—Fiction.
2. Peddlers and peddling—Fiction. 3. New York (N.Y.)—
Fiction. 4. War—Fiction] I. Solbert, Ronni, ill.
II. Title. III. Series.
PZ7.M54535Pu 1985   [Fic]   84-43131
ISBN 0-201-09313-8
ISBN 0-06-020822-8 (lib. bdg.)

FOREWORD

by Professor Lyman Cumberly of New York University,
author of *The Large Object Theory of History*

As the author says in her introduction, it is very important to the peace of the world that we understand how wars begin. Unfortunately, most of our modern wars are too big for the average person even to begin to understand. They take place on five continents at once. (One has to study geography for twenty years just to locate the battlefields.) They involve hundreds of armies, thousands of officers, millions of soldiers, and the weapons are so complicated that even the generals do not understand how they work.

The extraordinary thing about the Pushcart War is that a child of six will grasp at once precisely how the weapons worked. The Pushcart War is the only recent war of which this can be said.

The result is that we have been having more and more wars simply because the whole procedure is so complicated that peace-loving people give up trying to understand what is going on. This account of the Pushcart War should help to remedy this distressing situation. For big wars are caused by the same sort of problems that led to the Pushcart War.

Not that the Pushcart War was a small war. However, it *was* confined to the streets of one city, and it lasted only four months. During those four months, of course, the fate of one of the great cities of the world hung in the balance.

The author of this book is to be commended for her zeal in tracking down much behind-the-scenes material never before published. I, myself, had never heard the amusing story of Frank the

Flower's crocheted target, or the story behind Maxie Hammerman's capture of the bulletproof Italian car, a feat that demonstrates conclusively the brilliance of Maxie's strategy throughout the war.

Neither, I am ashamed to say, did I ever know the meaning of the inscription under General Anna's statue in Tompkins Square Park, although it is a park in which I spent many happy hours working on my *Large Object Theory of History*. (The author does not mention, I believe, that Tompkins Square Park was the battleground of another famous American war—but, of course, there are very few places left that have not been battlefields.)

I am sorry to say that I think the author may be mistaken about the number of pile driving firms in New York City at the time of the Pushcart War. She gives it as forty-three, although the *Pile Drivers' Annual* for that year lists fifty-three. A minor error in an otherwise impressive effort.

New York University
December 2, 1976

TABLE OF CONTENTS

INTRODUCTION

As it has been only ten years since the Pushcart War, I was surprised when one of my nephews a few months ago looked puzzled at the mention of a Mighty Mammoth. Then I realized that he had probably never seen a Mighty Mammoth. (He was only two at the time of the war and, moreover, was living in Iceland where his father had been sent on a government assignment.)

That a twelve-year-old boy might never have seen a Mighty Mammoth was understandable. What astonished me was that he had never even *heard* of one. But I have since discovered that there has never been a history of the Pushcart War written for young people.

Professor Lyman Cumberly's book, *The Large Object Theory of History,* drawn mainly from his observations of the Pushcart War, is a brilliant work. However, it is written primarily for college students.

I have always believed that we cannot have peace in the world until *all of us* understand how wars start. And so I have tried to set down the main events of the Pushcart War in such a way that readers of all ages may profit from whatever lessons it offers.

Although I was living in New York at the time of the war and saw the streets of New York overrun with Mighty Mammoths and Leaping Lemas, I did not then know any of the participants personally—except Buddy Wisser. I did contribute in a small way to the decisive battle described in Chapter XXXIV but, like most New Yorkers, was asleep in the early days of the war as to what was at issue—until Buddy Wisser alerted us all with his 160-by-160-foot enlargement of Marvin Seeley's photograph of the Daffodil Massacre.

Needless to say, Buddy Wisser has been a great help to me in the writing of this book. Buddy, before he became editor of one of New York's largest daily newspapers, had been sports editor of my high school newspaper, and at the time of the Pushcart War, Buddy and I ran into each other occasionally at Yankee Stadium.

It is to Buddy that I am indebted for the story behind the story of Marvin Seeley's picture. And it was through Buddy, of course, that I was able to meet many of the brave men and women who fought in the Pushcart War.

In addition to Buddy Wisser, I would like to express my appreciation to Maxie Hammerman for the many hours he spent answering my questions about his recollections of the war. Thanks, too, to Joey Kafflis for his permission to quote excerpts from his diary and to the New York Public Library's Rare Document Division for letting me see "The Portlette Papers."

Jean F. Merrill
Washington, Vt.
October 14, 1976

THE PUSHCART WAR

CHAPTER I

How It Began: The Daffodil Massacre

The Pushcart War started on the afternoon of March 15, 1986, when a truck ran down a pushcart belonging to a flower peddler. Daffodils were scattered all over the street. The pushcart was flattened, and the owner of the pushcart was pitched headfirst into a pickle barrel.

The owner of the cart was Morrie the Florist. The driver of the truck was Mack, who at the time was employed by Mammoth Moving. Mack's full name was Albert P. Mack, but in most accounts of the Pushcart War, he is referred to simply as Mack.

It was near the corner of Sixth Avenue and 17th Street in New York City that the trouble occurred. Mack was trying to park his truck. He had a load of piano stools to deliver, and the space in which he was hoping to park was not quite big enough.

When Mack saw that he could not get his truck into the space by the curb, he yelled at Morris the Florist to move his pushcart. Morris' cart was parked just ahead of Mack.

Morris had been parked in this spot for half an hour, and he was doing a good business. So he paid no attention to Mack. .

Mack pounded on his horn.

Morris looked up then. "Why should I move?" Morris asked. "I'm in business here."

Maybe if Mack had spoken courteously to Morris, Morris would have tried to push his cart forward a few feet. But Morris did not like being yelled at. He was a proud man. Besides, he had a customer.

So when Mack yelled again, "Move!" Morris merely shrugged.

"Move yourself," he said, and went on talking with his customer.

"Look, I got to unload ninety dozen piano stools before five o'clock," Mack said.

"I got to sell two dozen bunches of daffodils," Morris replied. "Tomorrow they won't be so fresh."

"In about two minutes they won't be so fresh," Mack said.

As several students of history have pointed out, Mack *could*

have simply nudged Morris' cart a bit with the fender of his truck. The truck was so much bigger than the pushcart that the slightest push would have rolled it forward. Not that Morris would have liked being pushed. Still, that was what truck drivers generally did when smaller vehicles were in their way.

But Mack was annoyed. Like most truck drivers of the time, he was used to having his own way. Mammoth Moving was one of the biggest trucking firms in the city, and Mack did not like a pushcart peddler arguing with him.

When Mack saw that Morris was not going to move, he backed up his truck. Morris heard him gunning his engine, but did not look around. He supposed Mack was going to drive on down the block. But instead of that, Mack drove straight into the back of Morris' pushcart. Daffodils were flung for a hundred feet and Morris himself, as we have said, was knocked into a pickle barrel. This was the event that we now know as the Daffodil Massacre.

These facts about the Daffodil Massacre are known because a boy, who had just been given a camera for his birthday, happened to be standing by the pickle barrel. His name was Marvin Seeley.

CHAPTER II

The Blow-up of Marvin Seeley's Picture

Marvin Seeley had been trying, on the afternoon of March 15th, to take a picture of a pickle barrel which stood in front of a grocery store on 17th Street. Marvin had been annoyed to have a man go flying into the barrel at the very instant he snapped the picture. However, when the picture was developed, the daffodils came out so nicely that Marvin sent the picture to a magazine that was having a contest.

Although the magazine preferred pictures of plain pickle barrels to pictures of accidents, the picture won an Honorable Mention and was printed in the magazine where a newspaper editor's wife, named Emily Wisser, happened to see it. Emily, who was fond of flowers, cut out the picture for a scrapbook she kept.

Later, when everyone began arguing about how the Pushcart War had started, Emily remembered Marvin Seeley's picture and showed it to her husband. Emily's husband, Buddy Wisser, had always laughed at his wife's scrapbooks, but for once he was very interested. As editor of one of the city's largest papers, he could not afford to laugh off a good story.

From Marvin Seeley's picture, Buddy Wisser was able to track down a good many facts. For one thing, he was able to identify the owner of the pushcart as Morris the Florist (although you cannot see Morris' face in the picture, as his head is well down in the pickle barrel).

Mack's face, however, is clearly visible, as is the name of the trucking company. Mack is leaning from his cab window and scowling, and MAMMOTH MOVING is printed in large letters on the side of the truck.

Mammoth was a well-known trucking firm. The firm owned seventy-two trucks at the time. Its slogan was: "If It Is a Big Job, Why Not Make It a MAMMOTH Job?"

Mammoth trucks came in three sizes. There were the Number One's, or "Baby Mammoths," as the drivers called them. There were the Number Two's, or "Mama Mammoths," and there were the Number Three's, the "Mighty Mammoths." It was a Mighty Mammoth that ran down Morris the Florist.

There was a lot of argument about the size of Mack's truck until Buddy Wisser decided to have Marvin Seeley's picture enlarged. Buddy Wisser had the picture blown up until Mack's face was life-size, and when Mack's face was life-size, the pickle barrel and the daffodils and the truck were all life-size, too. Then all Buddy Wisser had to do was to take a tape measure and measure the truck.

Not that this was easy. The enlarged picture was so large that Buddy Wisser had to go to a park near his office and lay the picture on the ground in order to measure the truck. It was a Mighty Mammoth, all right.

It was this big picture that also gave Buddy Wisser the clue he needed to identify the owner of the pushcart. In the lower

left-hand corner of the picture, Buddy observed several splintered bits of the pushcart. On one of these fragments, he made out the letters "ORRIS," and on another—"ORIST."

Buddy Wisser's enlargement of Marvin Seeley's picture now hangs in the Museum of the City of New York. The Museum preserved the picture, partly because its size makes it a curiosity, and partly because it is a historical document. It is the best proof we have of how the Pushcart War actually began.

CHAPTER III

More About Morris the Florist & A Little About Frank
the Flower and Maxie Hammerman, the Pushcart King

At the time of the Pushcart War, Morris the Florist had
been in the flower line for forty-three years. He was a soft-
spoken man, and his only claim to fame before the war was
that it was impossible to buy a dozen flowers from him.

If a customer asked Morris for a dozen tulips—or daffodils
or mixed snapdragons—Morris always wrapped up thirteen
flowers. The one extra was at no cost. "So it shouldn't be a
small dozen," Morris said.

Morris sold his flowers from a pushcart which he pushed

between Sixth and Seventh Avenues from 14th Street to 23rd Street. He never went above 23rd. It was not that he didn't like it farther uptown, but above 23rd was Frank the Flower's territory.

Frank the Flower and Morris the Florist were not close friends before the Pushcart War, but they respected each other. Frank was the first to chip in to help buy Morris a new pushcart after Mack ran him down.

Anyone who knew Morris in those days found it hard to imagine him provoking a war. It would be closer to the truth to say that for a long time there had been trouble coming, and that Morris the Florist just happened to be standing on the corner of Sixth Avenue and 17th Street the afternoon it came.

For a long time New York had been one of the largest cities in the world. New Yorkers had long been proud that their streets were busier and noisier and more crowded than anyone else's.

Visitors to New York would say, "It's nice, but it's so crowded."

To which New Yorkers would reply cheerfully, "Yes, it's about the most crowded city in the world." And the city had kept on growing.

Every year there were more automobiles. More taxis. More buses. More trucks. Especially more trucks. By the summer of the Pushcart War, there were more trucks in New York than anyplace in the world.

There were also some five hundred pushcarts, though few people had any idea that there were more than a hundred or so. Probably only Maxie Hammerman really knew how many pushcarts there were.

Maxie knew, because Maxie or Maxie's father or Maxie's grandfather had built most of the pushcarts in New York. Maxie had a shop where he built and repaired pushcarts. It was the same shop in which his father and grandfather had started building pushcarts.

Maxie Hammerman knew the license number of almost every pushcart licensed to do business in New York. If you said to Maxie, "Morris the Florist," Maxie would come right back at you, "X-105," which was Morris' license number.

Also, Maxie was very nice about giving business advice. If a peddler came to Maxie and asked him to build a pushcart for a fresh-vegetable line, Maxie would think the matter over and then he would ask the peddler where he planned to push the cart.

If the peddler said, "East of Tompkins Square, north to

14th and south to Delancey," Maxie would run over his license list in his head and say, "Already there are thirteen carts in the fresh-vegetable line in that territory. Maybe you could push some other line?"

Maxie's advice was usually very sound, and he was known to his friends and to the peddlers who bought their carts from him as the Pushcart King. Very few people except Maxie's friends and the pushcart peddlers even knew there was a push-cart king.

CHAPTER IV

The Summer Before the War

Certainly there had been trouble coming. Anyone who had had any experience of wars would have seen it coming long before the afternoon that Mack ran down Morris the Florist.

There had been general grumbling. New York had become so crowded with cars and taxis and buses and trucks that traffic was very slow.

At first, everyone blamed everyone else. People who drove their own cars grumbled about people who rode in taxis. If there were no taxis, said the automobile owners, there would be room to drive in the streets.

Taxi drivers, on the other hand, complained about people who drove their own cars. If private cars were kept off the streets, people could get where they wanted to go in a hurry, the taxi drivers claimed.

The bus drivers suggested that both the taxis and the private cars should get off the streets. And the people who liked to walk found fault with everything on wheels.

But what irritated *everyone* were the trucks. There were so many of them, and they were so big that they did not have to get out of the way for anyone.

Most of the businesses in the city hired trucks to carry their goods from one place to another. To get an idea of how many trucks there were on the streets at the time, one may turn to the telephone book for that year.

In the classified section, for instance, if one opens to the "P" listings, a few of the products one will find advertised there are:

Package Handles
Paint
Pajama Trimmings
Pancake Mixes
Pants
Paper Plates
Parachutes
Park Benches
Parking Meters
Parquet Floors
Party Favors
Paste
Patent Medicines
Patterns
Paving Brick
Pawn Tickets
Peas
Peanut Butter
Pearls

Pecans
Pencils
Pen Knives
Penicillin
Pennants
Pens
Pepper
Perambulators
Percales
Perfumes
Periodicals
Permanent Wave Machines
Pet Shop Supplies
Petroleum
Pewter
Pharmaceuticals
Phonographs
Photographic Supplies
Piano Stools
Piccolos
Pickle Barrels
Picnic Tables
Picture Frames
Picture Post Cards
Picture Windows

Pies
Pigskins
Pile Drivers
Pillows
Pins
Pipe
Pipe Organs
Pistol Belts
Piston Rings
Pizza Pie Supplies
Place Cards
Planetariums
Plant Foods
Plaques
Plaster of Paris
Plastics
Plate Glass
Platforms
Platinum
Playground Equipment
Playing Cards
Playsuits
Playthings
Pleating Machine Parts
Plexiglass
Pliers
Plows
Plugs
Plumbago
Plushes
Plywood
Pocketbooks
Podiums
Poker Chips
Poisons
Poles
Police Badges

Polish
Polo Mallets
Pompoms
Ponchos
Pony Carts
Pool Tables
Popcorn Machines
Porch Furniture
Postage Stamp Affixers
Posters
Potatoes
Potato Peelers
Pot Holders
Potted Plants
Pottery
Poultry
Powder Puffs
Precious Stones
Precision Castings
Premium Goods
Preserves
Pressing Machines
Pressure Cookers
Pretzels
Price Tags
Printing Presses
Propellers
Projectors
Prunes
Public Address Systems
Publications
Pulleys
Pulpits
Pumice
Pumps
Punch Bowls
Puppets

Purses
Pushcart Parts
Putty
Puzzles

One must keep in mind that the products mentioned above are only a *few* of the things listed under the letter "P". Consider, too, that the phone book lists not only pile drivers, for example, but forty-three *different* firms in the pile-driving business (not to mention the *7234!* different firms in the plastics business). Then, if one remembers that *each* of those forty-three firms employed on the average of seventeen and a half trucks a day, one will begin to get an idea of the number of trucks that there must have been in New York just before the Pushcart War.

The worst of it was that during the period that more and more trucks had been appearing in the city streets, the trucks had been getting bigger and bigger. The truck drivers had it all figured out.

At least, that is what Professor Lyman Cumberly, of New York University, said when he was writing about the Pushcart War some years later. Professor Cumberly's notion was that the truck drivers had gotten together and figured out that in crowded traffic conditions, the only way to get where you wanted to go was to be *so* big that you didn't have to get out of the way for anybody. This is known as the Large Object Theory of History.

CHAPTER V

Wenda Gambling Sees the Danger Signs

It is a matter of historical record that the average truck in New York City at the time of the Pushcart War was so big that no one driving behind it could see around it to check the names of the streets he was passing. Wenda Gambling, a well-known movie star, on her way to 96th Street to visit her ninety-year-old grandmother, once got stuck behind a gasoline truck.

For all her experience in the movies, Wenda was a timid driver and was afraid the truck would explode if she tried to pass it. It had big red DANGER signs painted all over it, Wenda recalls.

Since Wenda did not dare pass the truck, and since she could not see any street signs, she not only went past 96th Street, but was at Bear Mountain, some fifty miles beyond the city limits, before she had any idea where she was. By then, of course, she was so frightened that she had to spend the night in a log cabin in Harriman State Park.

A search party did not find her until 6:30 the following morning. She had not had anything to eat but some dry oatmeal that someone had left in the cabin.

This kind of thing kept happening. Wenda's case is remembered, because Wenda's activities were always reported in the headlines. But other people ran into similar troubles.

More and more the truck drivers crowded other drivers to the sides of the street. They hogged the best parking places. Or, if there were no parking places, and a truck driver felt like having a cup of coffee, he simply stopped his truck in the middle of the street and left it there, blocking the traffic for miles behind him.

The heavier the traffic, the ruder the truck drivers became. At busy intersections, they never let anyone else turn first. If anyone tried to, a truck driver had only to gun his engine and keep on coming. Few automobile drivers cared to argue with a twelve-ton truck, even when they were in the right.

Even the taxi drivers began to lose their confidence. For a long time the taxis had been considered a match for the trucks because of the daring, speed, and skill of their drivers. When the taxi drivers grew cautious, many people were alarmed.

CHAPTER VI

The Peanut Butter Speech

One of the first people to speak out against the growing danger was a man named Archie Love. Archie Love was running for Mayor at the time, and he promised to reduce the number of trucks in the streets.

It looked briefly as if Archie Love might be elected on the strength of this promise alone. But that was before Archie's opponent, Emmett P. Cudd (who was already Mayor and did not want to lose his job), made his famous "Peanut Butter Speech" in Union Square.

Mayor Cudd repeated the Peanut Butter Speech ninety times in one week. It went more or less as follows:

"Friends and New Yorkers: New York is one of the biggest cities in the U.S.A. We are proud of that fact.

"What makes a city big? Big business, naturally.

"And what is the difference between big business and small business? It is this: If you order fourteen cartons of peanut butter, you are running a small business. If you order four hundred cartons of peanut butter, you are running a big business.

"Fourteen cartons of peanut butter, you can get delivered in a station wagon. But for four hundred cartons of peanut butter, you need a truck. And you need a *big* truck. Big trucks mean progress.

"My opponent, Archie Love, is against trucks. He is, therefore, against progress. Maybe he is even against peanut butter."

33

Naturally, all the truck drivers voted to re-elect Mayor Cudd, and so did a lot of other people. Very few people wanted to be against progress. No one wanted to be against peanut butter. And *everyone* wanted to be proud of their city, because they always had been. Thus, Archie Love did not get elected, and the trucks kept getting bigger.

As the trucks increased in size, traffic—as Archie Love had predicted—grew steadily worse until, in the spring before the Pushcart War, the city was one big traffic jam most of the time. One day it took a taxi four hours to drive five blocks.

The passenger in the taxi was Professor Lyman Cumberly, who did not complain because he was working on his Large Object Theory of History and found the situation interesting from a scientific point of view. During this ride, Professor Cumberly fell into conversation with an impatient young man from Seattle who was trapped in an adjoining taxi.

The young man was shocked that so many New Yorkers accepted the terrible conditions in their streets without protest, and Professor Cumberly recalls that the visitor had very definite ideas what should be done about the trucks. In fact, encouraged by Professor Cumberly's interest, the young man flew back to Seattle and wrote a book.

The book, called *The Enemy in the Streets,* was a fearless attack on the trucks. However, as the author was unknown, the book did not receive much notice at the time it was published. It is remembered today largely because the author is now President of the United States.

CHAPTER VII

The Words That Triggered the War
(Wenda Gambling's Innocent Remark)

What finally brought matters to a head was a television program called "The Day the Traffic Stopped." The day before the program, the traffic *had* stopped entirely, and one of the television stations had hurriedly called in a panel of experts to explain why.

The members of the panel were:

Robert Alexander Wrightson—Traffic Commissioner of New York

Alexander P. Wolfson—head of Wolfson & Wolfson, specialists in traffic coordination

Dr. Wolfe Alexander—a traffic psychologist

Wenda Gambling—a well-known movie star

Wenda Gambling was hardly an expert on traffic. But as the three other panel members were elderly men (one stout, one bald, and one near-sighted), the moderator of the program felt that the panel would be more interesting to the audience if Wenda were at the table.

In introducing Wenda, the moderator of the program said, "As we all know, Miss Gambling's new movie, *The Streets of New York,* is being shot on the streets of New York, and as the streets of New York are the subject of our discussion tonight, it is very appropriate that she should be here."

Wenda tactfully left most of the talking to the experts. Each of the three men had a different theory as to why the traffic had stopped.

Robert Alexander Wrightson said that there was no cause for alarm, that the whole thing was a simple matter of what he liked to call "the density of moving objects."

Alexander P. Wolfson disagreed. He said the problem involved nothing more than "a predictable increase in the number of unmoving objects."

Dr. Wolfe Alexander said that it did not matter whether the objects were moving or unmoving as the whole thing could be easily solved by "a more thorough conditioning of drivers to hopeless situations."

"And what do you think, Miss Gambling?" asked the moderator, as the three experts began to argue with each other.

"I don't know what they are talking about," said Wenda Gambling.

"Well," said the moderator, who was not quite sure himself, "I believe our subject this evening was traffic."

"Oh," said Wenda Gambling. "Well, I think that there are too many trucks and that the trucks are too big."

Since most of the television audience had been watching Wenda Gambling rather than the experts—and since everyone watching *did* know what Wenda was talking about—this one remark received more attention than anything else that was said on the program. Before the program was off the air, over five thousand viewers had called the station to say that they agreed with Wenda Gambling.

Professor Lyman Cumberly has suggested that except for Wenda Gambling's innocent remark, there might never have been a Pushcart War. Instead, says Professor Cumberly, the trucks would have simply gone on taking over the city, crowding out the taxis, buses, cars—and finally the people themselves. No one would have challenged them until it was too late.

It would, Professor Cumberly believes, have been the end of life in New York as we know it. But once Wenda Gambling had stated the danger for all to hear, war was inevitable.

CHAPTER VIII

The Secret Meeting & The Declaration of War
(Excerpts from the Diary of Joey Kafflis)

The truck drivers themselves were the first to grasp the meaning of the widespread response to Wenda Gambling's remark. The day after the television program, representatives of all the trucking firms in the city held a secret meeting.

The meeting was organized by "The Three," as the owners of the three largest trucking firms in the city were called. The Three were Moe Mammoth (of Mammoth Moving)—or "Big Moe," as his drivers called him, Walter Sweet, of Tiger Trucking (who preferred to be known as "The Tiger") and Louie Livergreen of LEMA (Lower Eastside Moving Association).

The plotting of the Pushcart War and the truckers' strategy throughout was, for the most part, the work of The Three.* Big Moe generally served as spokesman for The Three, and it was Big Moe who presided over the secret meeting.

---

* "The Three" were originally known as "The Big Three," but this caused some confusion as the leaders of three important nations of the time were also called The Big Three, and after a city newspaper ran a headline announcing BIG THREE CARVE UP CHINA (over a story about Mammoth, LEMA, and Tiger Trucking buying out the China Carting & Storage Co.), there was some international trouble in the course of which Moscow was bombed b... Indo-Chinese pilot. After that the city papers referred to the three b... firms simply as The Three.

The meeting was held in an underground garage owned by Mammoth Moving. It was at this meeting that a young truck driver named Joey Kafflis had the nerve to stand up and say, "People are right. Traffic is lousy, and there *are* too many trucks."

Joey, who worked for Tiger Trucking, was fired shortly after this meeting. Fortunately, Joey kept a diary. The diary was something that he had started to pass the time when his truck was stalled in a traffic jam. It is from this diary that we have a first-hand account of what happened at the first secret meeting and in the days that followed.

Here are some excerpts from Joey Kafflis' diary, dated the day after the secret meeting:

February 15. Columbus Avenue and 66th Street en route to 9th and 86th with two dozen pipe organs. 11:15 A.M.

It looks like a long tie-up ahead, so I may as well put down a few more facts about the meeting last night. After I have said, "Traffic is lousy," there is a big silence. Everybody looks at me very surprised, and several guys look as if I have hurt their feelings.

Then Big Moe, who is running the meeting, gets up and growls. By that I mean that he clears his throat in a particular way Big Moe has of clearing his throat. It is as if you were racing your engine a little bit to test whether you have the power and the engine is warmed up.

"Now maybe traffic is not so good," Big Moe says. For a minute I think he is going to agree with me. But instead he glares at me and says—and he is nicely warmed up by now—"*I say,* Mr. Kafflis, that is all a question of who is to blame for the traffic situation. Why pick on the poor trucks?"

When Big Moe says "poor trucks," I laugh out loud. But nobody hears me, because everybody is cheering for Big Moe. . . .

12:15 P.M. *Columbus Avenue and 69th Street.*

I thought I was going to make 86th Street by lunch time, but there is still trouble up ahead. So I will continue.

After Big Moe says "poor trucks," a trucker named Little Miltie stands up. Little Miltie says, "I agree with Big Moe. Why blame the poor trucks? If you ask me, it is all those pushcarts that are blocking the streets."

Nobody likes this Little Miltie too much, as he is known as a very mean driver. By that I mean that Little Miltie would crowd out another truck as soon as he would a taxi. But for once Little Miltie gets a big hand, and about ten different truck drivers then begin to tell how slow the pushcarts are, and how pushcarts are always sitting by the curb where a trucker wants to park, and how pushcarts should not be allowed to take up space in a modern city like New York.

Once more I have to laugh, and this time everyone hears me. So I explain, "Come on—how much room do a few pushcarts take?" Because I personally do not mind the pushcarts.

When I am stuck in traffic like today (like almost any day, for that matter), a pushcart will come along and sell me a sausage roll, which passes the time. You get the best sausage rolls around Thompson Street. Sixty-ninth, where I am now, is not too good for sausage rolls.

It looks like something is moving up ahead, so I will put this away until another time.

Columbus Avenue and 75th Street. 4:05 P.M.

Now there is a trailer-truck backed up to the curb at 76th. It is sticking halfway out into the street. The taxi driver ahead of me says that they are unloading permanent wave machines, and that it will be a half-hour tie-up, at least. So I may as well finish writing about the secret meeting while it is still fresh in my mind. I left off with how I was speaking up for the pushcarts.

"Come on," I say, "how much room do a few pushcarts take?" I address my question to a driver named Mack.

"You could line up two dozen pushcarts along the curb before those carts would take up one-half the space of a truck like a Mighty Mammoth," I point out to Mack. Mack drives a Mighty Mammoth.

"Or, a Ten-Ton Tiger," I say, putting myself in the same spot. When I mention a Ten-Ton Tiger, Big Moe looks at my boss.

42

My boss is Mr. Walter Sweet, who is sitting right beside Big Moe, as he is one of The Three.

Big Moe asks Walter Sweet, "Does this boy drive for Tiger Trucking?"—a silly question, as I have as much as said I drive a Ten-Ton Tiger. And the boss has to admit I do.

I am sorry if I have embarrassed the boss. Mr. Walter Sweet has a kind heart for the most part.

"Do you have anything more to say, Mr. Kafflis?" Big Moe asks me. And he asks me in such a tone of voice that I know he is telling me he could be helpful in helping me to lose my job with Tiger Trucking.

However, I am not afraid of Big Moe. It occurred to me a long time ago that there are so many reasons you could lose a job that if you started to worry about them all, you would be afraid to say anything. And for anyone who has a lot to say, as I do, this would be a hardship.

However, I shut up for the simple reason that I do not have anything else to say at the moment. It is such a nutty argument about the pushcarts.

The next speaker at the meeting is Louie Livergreen. Louie owns all those Leaping Lemas on the Lower East Side and has pretty well cut everybody else out of business down there.

Now Louie speaks in a very smooth way. He is not a pleasant-looking man, but he speaks in a smooth voice. I have noticed that each of The Three speaks in a different way.

Big Moe speaks in a loud voice—"a voice like a truck driver," my sister once said, which I felt was an insulting remark. But many people think of truck drivers in this way.

The Tiger, on the other hand, has a low voice. And Louie Livergreen, on the third hand, speaks—as I mentioned—in a smooth voice.

Of The Three, it is Louie Livergreen that I would be afraid of, and I think that is because his voice is as smooth as a good grade of motor oil, whether he is saying something perfectly pleasant or something terrible. If somebody says something terrible in a pleasant tone of voice, I get very nervous. I would feel better if they yelled.

Well, as I said, Louie Livergreen starts to talk to the drivers in that smooth voice. "Our boys are telling us that the pushcarts are ruining the city," Louie says.

"And believe me, I am glad that you have been so frank about the trouble. Mr. Mammoth and Mr. Sweet and myself are not out in the trucks so much ourselves, and we have to rely on our boys to give us the facts.

"And now that we have got the facts," says Louie, "it is very clear what we have got to do."

Louie explains that what we have got to do is to educate the public. "When people complain about the traffic," he says, "we have got to tell the people who is to blame. Otherwise, they will be blaming the trucks."

44

From the tone of his voice and the respectful way the truck drivers are listening to him, Louie could be delivering a sermon in a church, which is not exactly the case.

"I know what you boys are up against," Louie goes on to say. "I operate on the East Side where most of the pushcarts also operate. And I know these people. They are behind the times and a danger to the rest of us, and they have got to go."

Louie gets a big hand at this point, but he is not finished. "I will tell you something else," he says. "And it is not something I am proud of. My own father was a pushcart peddler, and if I had not had the guts to get out and fight for myself, no matter who was in my way, I might be pushing a pushcart myself.

"Instead," Louie points out, "I have built up the firm of LEMA and put one hundred Leaping Lemas on the streets every day of the year, rain or shine. And that I am proud of!"

Louie gets a big hand again. Not from me, though. While I agree that one hundred trucks is something to be proud of, I do not see why a man wants to talk as Louie is talking about his father—who maybe did not have such an easy time, and rain or shine, is out in the streets with a pushcart. Whereas Louie— if it rains—can send out one hundred drivers.

Louie has a few other remarks. Mainly this one: "I think you boys know that the Lower Eastside Moving Association has been working on a Master Plan for the streets of New York, a plan that will greatly improve the situation for truck drivers. I have discussed this plan with Mr. Moe Mammoth and Mr. Walter Sweet, and the plan is moving forward nicely. But before it can go into effect, we have got to solve the pushcart problem."

I have not heard about this Master Plan of Louie Livergreen's before, but all around me drivers are nodding as if it is a fine idea.

I ask several of the boys about it, and they say it is probably the usual thing—to make things better for the truckers in the streets and maybe more money for the drivers.

I don't know about the Master Plan, but it seems to me that the idea of the meeting is that The Three are declaring war on the pushcarts.

Well, I must sign off now, as the taxi driver ahead is signaling that they have got those permanent wave machines off the trailer. Unfortunately, I see that it is 5:30, so I will have to take the pipe organs back to the warehouse and try to get to 86th Street tomorrow.* Really, traffic *is* lousy."

---

* Joey Kafflis never did get to deliver the pipe organs that he was transporting on February 15. The following day he was fired, and the rest of his diary is concerned with a potato farm on eastern Long Island that he acquired shortly thereafter.

CHAPTER IX

The Secret Campaign Against the Pushcarts

The Pushcart War is generally divided into two major campaigns. The first of these is referred to as the Secret Campaign. For although we now have the evidence of the Kafflis diary that The Three *had* declared war on the pushcarts at the secret meeting, this declaration was not at the time made public. This gave the trucks an enormous advantage in the beginning.

The pushcart peddlers themselves did not know for over a month that the truckers had declared war on them. All they knew was that suddenly the truck drivers were nudging their pushcarts out of the way more and more often, and that they were nudging harder and harder.

In one week alone, more than one hundred carts were brought into Maxie Hammerman's for repairs. Maxie repaired broken slatting, broken spokes, broken handles, and bent axles. Many of the pushcarts had to be entirely rebuilt, and Maxie did not have time to build any new carts. Also, the number of serious accidents involving pushcarts increased, and several peddlers needed hospital treatment for broken legs or crushed ribs.

At first, the pushcart peddlers thought that all these troubles were simply a case of the already terrible traffic conditions getting rapidly worse. Then they began to hear puzzling remarks from people standing on street corners. Whenever someone complained about the traffic, there was always someone else on hand to say, "I hear it is the pushcarts that are to blame."

People always said, "I *hear.*" Where they had heard, nobody was sure.

A great many of the rumors probably came from readers of a weekly newspaper called *The Ears & Eyes of the Lower East Side.* This paper was published as a community service by LEMA (Lower Eastside Moving Association). *The Ears & Eyes* was given away free to grocery stores to pass on to their customers. It was also sent free to members of the City Council and other important people.

In *The Ears & Eyes,* there was a regular column by a man who signed himself "The Community Reporter." The Community Reporter wrote a great many columns just before the war about what he called "The Pushcart Menace."

The Community Reporter reported that "people" wanted to get rid of the pushcarts in order to make the streets of the city safer and more attractive. He said that "people" said that the pushcarts were "unsound and unsanitary."

The Community Reporter was always telling people about what "people" wanted. Before he began writing about The Pushcart Menace, he wrote about trees. He said that "people" also wanted to get rid of the trees planted along the sidewalks of the city so that the streets could be wider and more attractive. He said that trees were unsanitary, too, because leaves were always falling on the sidewalk.

The Community Reporter said that people thought the streets should be wider and more attractive, even if it meant getting rid of the sidewalks and some of the houses and schools and churches and small candy stores. Many of these were unsound and unsanitary anyway, he said.

However, in the spring before the war, it was mainly the pushcarts that the Community Reporter wrote about. He made it sound as if pushcarts were even more unsound and unsanitary than trees, houses, schools, churches, and candy stores.

It is uncertain how many people read *The Ears & Eyes*. (Some grocers said that they had trouble giving it away, as most of their customers did not mind a few leaves falling off trees.) But enough people did see the Community Reporter's column for one of the more respectable daily papers to announce a series entitled: "Pushcarts—Are They a Menace to Our Streets?"

As part of this series, a reporter interviewed Moe Mammoth. This was the day after a Mama Mammoth had upset three vegetable carts on Avenue C.

"That poor Mama," said Big Moe. "Tomatoes all over the street, and twenty pushcart peddlers yelling at the truck driver, and picking up broken tomatoes and throwing them at him. What kind of working conditions are those?"

"Are you saying the pushcarts *are* a menace?" asked the reporter.

"The facts speak for themselves," said Big Moe. "As a public service, Mr. Louie Livergreen, of the Lower Eastside Moving Association—which has one hundred trucks out on the streets every day—has made a count of the number of accidents involving pushcarts in the last month.

"In the last month alone," Big Moe said, "Mr. Livergreen tells me there have been one hundred and forty-one *more* pushcart accidents than in the month before.

"My own drivers," Big Moe added, "have orders to report every pushcart accident they see, and they say that they are held up by pushcarts several times a day."

"And you think that these accidents are tying up the traffic?" asked the reporter.

"That is what my drivers say," said Big Moe. "Of course, we all know the pushcarts are not designed for modern traffic conditions."

When Maxie Hammerman read that last remark, he was so angry that he threw a hammer through his own shop window. "Not *designed!*" he roared at Frank the Flower, who had stopped by Maxie's shop to have a few bolts tightened on his cart.

"Someone is saying that a pushcart is not *designed?* A pushcart is *perfectly* designed," Maxie said, glowering at his broken window.

"Look now," he said, slapping the side of Frank the Flower's cart. "Look how compact. So it shouldn't take up too much space in a crowded street."

"I am not complaining," said Frank the Flower.

"*Designed,*" growled Maxie Hammerman, normally a pleasant-tempered man. He was really very insulted.

50

"Designed," Maxie went on, "—what I would like to get my hands on designing is Mr. Moe Mammoth. I give you my word, when I'm finished, he will be designed very much smaller."

Maxie Hammerman was not the only one to take offense at Big Moe's remarks. All the pushcart peddlers were angry at Big Moe's blaming the accidents on them.

"Because the pushcarts are *in* the accidents, does it mean we *caused* them?" asked Eddie Moroney, whose cart was not only well-designed, but beautifully lettered—"Coal & Ice—Home Delivered." (Eddie Moroney had lettered circus carts and posters before he went into business for himself.)

"Since when did a pushcart hit a truck?" Eddie demanded.

"Believe me, it would give me pleasure," said Frank the Flower.

"What I don't like is 'unsanitary,'" said Old Anna, who sold apples and pears of the best quality outside hospitals and museums.

"What is this *unsanitary* I am hearing about?" Old Anna demanded. "My cart is as clean as a teacup I would drink from. How can I be unsanitary in front of hospitals? What do they mean 'unsanitary'?"

"Plastic bags, maybe," said Frank the Flower. "In the supermarkets, they put the apples and pears in plastic bags."

"Plastic!" said Old Anna. "So you can't examine the fruit. That is why they have plastic bags."

"But people think it is more sanitary," said Frank the Flower.

"Sanitary!" said Old Anna. "Who sees whether the man who puts the fruit in the plastic bags has washed his hands?"

"Every customer can see for himself that my hands are clean," said Old Anna. "You put apples in a plastic bag in the back room of a store—and who *knows*?

"Also," said Old Anna, "I have noticed that apples in a plastic bag are two pounds for twenty-nine cents. In a paper bag, such as I use, they are three pounds for twenty-nine.

"You ask me what is the menace," said Old Anna. "And I will tell you. It is *plastic bags!*"

CHAPTER X

The Meeting at Maxie Hammerman's: **The Pushcarts**
Decide to Fight

Looking back on the Pushcart War, it seems possible that the trucks might have gone on slowly breaking up the pushcarts in what looked like accidents, if it had not been for Mack's brutal attack on Morris the Florist. But the day after Mack hit Morris, the pushcart peddlers held a meeting at Maxie Hammerman's shop. It was at this meeting that the peddlers decided to fight back.

The meeting had been called to take up a collection to buy Morris the Florist a new cart. Peddlers from all over the city were there.

Every kind of pushcart business was represented—hot dogs and sauerkraut, roast chestnuts, old clothes, ice and coal, ices and ice cream sticks, fruit and vegetables, used cartons, shoe laces and combs, pretzels, dancing dolls, and nylon stockings, to mention only a few. Most of the peddlers who became well-known to the public during the Pushcart War were present at this meeting.

Old Anna ("Apples and Pears") was there. So was Mr. Jerusalem ("All Kinds Junk—Bought & Sold"). Harry the Hot Dog ("Harry's Hots & Homemade Sauerkraut") was there. Carlos ("Cartons Flattened and Removed") was there. Eddie Moroney ("Coal & Ice—Home Delivered"—lettered

in three colors) was there. Papa Peretz ("Pretzels—6 for 25¢") was there.

Frank the Flower, of course, was there. He was the first to speak. It was Frank the Flower's idea to take up a collection to buy Morris a new cart.

"As you can see from the bandage on his head, my friend Morris has had a terrible experience," said Frank the Flower. "Worse yet, his cart is ruined."

"It is a fact," said Maxie Hammerman. "I could not put that cart together in one hundred years."

"What I wish to point out," said Frank the Flower, "is this: Today it is Morris they are putting out of business. Tomorrow it may be you or me. I think we should every one of us give ten cents—maybe fifteen—so that Morris can buy a new cart. If it happened to us, Morris would do the same."

"Believe me, I would," said Morris. "But I pray it shouldn't happen to anyone else."

Mr. Jerusalem ("All Kinds Junk—Bought & Sold") stood

up. "The ten cents we will give," he said. "Or fifteen. No question. What I want to know is why they are breaking us up. All of a sudden—accidents."

"*Accidents!*" said Old Anna. "Is it an accident that Morris the Florist has had? Accidents on purpose, that is what is happening."

"All right—on purpose," Mr. Jerusalem agreed. "But *why?*" he demanded.

"They are telling everybody we are in the way," said Papa Peretz ("Pretzels—6 for 25¢"). "I hear it on 14th Street. I hear it on 23rd. Even on Delancey Street I hear it. Everywhere, they are saying that we are in the way."

"*Way!*" said Old Anna. "Whose way am I in? I am quiet about my business. I don't take up much space. For forty-five years I sell my apples in front of hospitals, museums, and the best downtown offices. My customers ask about my health—my family. It is the first time I hear that I am in the way. *Whose* way?"

Maxie Hammerman got up then. "I will explain," said Maxie, who had been doing some serious thinking since the day he threw his hammer through his own shop window.

"Conditions are very bad in the streets," Maxie said. "People are getting mad at the trucks. They should have got mad a long time ago. But everybody was scared. Who wants to argue with a truck?

"However, there comes a time," Maxie said. "People begin to complain, and the trucks do not want the blame for tying up the streets. So they have to find somebody else to blame.

"Who shall they blame?" Maxie asked. "Taxis? No, there are too many taxis. Cars? No, too many cars. The trucks do not want to fight the cars and the taxis. That would make too many *more* people mad at them. But pushcarts—how many are there?"

"There are hundreds of pushcarts," said Harry the Hot Dog ("Harry's Hots & Homemade Sauerkraut").

"Five hundred and nine, to be exact," said Maxie Hammerman. "More than most people think, because pushcarts stay in their own neighborhoods. They are not rushing all over the city to make the traffic worse. Stop a man on the street and ask him how many pushcarts has he seen today. He will tell you, 'Three—maybe four' —although there are five hundred and nine carts licensed to do business in this city.

"However," Maxie added. "Even five hundred and nine is a small number beside taxis and cars."

"I don't understand," said Papa Peretz. "they could kill us all, and the traffic would still be terrible."

"So then they will have to find someone else to blame," said Maxie Hammerman. "Motorcycles, maybe. Or grocery carts, such as the ladies take to the supermarket. Then people will see how silly it is."

"By then," said Old Anna," we will all be dead."

"That is correct," said Maxie Hammerman. "We will all be dead. Unless—" Maxie picked up a hammer and held it as if he were about to hit something a quick hard blow.

"Unless what?" said Frank the Flower, seizing Maxie's arm, in case he should be about to throw the hammer through his window again.

"Unless we fight back," said Maxie Hammerman, pulling his arm free and whamming the hammer down on the table in front of him. "I say the pushcarts have got to fight."

"Of course, we have got to fight," said Old Anna.

"Fight the trucks?" said Papa Peretz. "How can the pushcarts fight the trucks?"

"Maybe you'd rather be dead?" said Old Anna.

"Naturally, we wouldn't," said Harry the Hot Dog. "But how can we fight the trucks?"

"Listen to me, Harry," said Old Anna. *"First,* you decide to fight. Then you ask me how."

"All right," said Harry the Hot Dog. "Fight! So now I ask you—how?"

"Yes, General Anna, we are listening," said Eddie Moroney, bowing to Old Anna. (This is how Old Anna came to be known as General Anna. Eddie Moroney called her General at the meeting at Maxie Hammerman's shop, and the name seemed to suit her.)

When it came to a vote, all the pushcart peddlers were with General Anna. They realized that they had to stick together. And they had to fight.

"But how?" Harry the Hot Dog asked again. "You want me to sell poison hot dogs to all the truck drivers maybe?"

General Anna shook her head. "It's okay by me you should poison the truck drivers. Only you might get the poison dogs mixed up with the regular, and then you'll be giving the poison to a good customer."

"We need a secret weapon," said Papa Peretz. "Like a big bomb."

"For carrying around bombs, you get arrested," said General Anna.

To everyone's surprise, it was Carlos ("Cartons Flattened and Removed") who had the best idea. Carlos had never spoken out in a meeting before.

CHAPTER XI

The Secret Weapon

Carlos was known to the pushcart peddlers as the most skillful carton-flattener in the Lower East Side section of New York City. Carlos' business was to go around to small stores that had clean cardboard cartons which they wished to be rid of. With two or three deft motions, Carlos would flatten the cartons and carefully stack them on his pushcart. Carlos was the only flattener in the business who could stack to a height of twelve feet without the cartons slipping off.

When he had a load, Carlos would deliver the cartons to another small business that needed a few cartons. This was a very practical business as Carlos did not have to pay out any money for the goods he sold. The storekeepers were glad to get rid of the cartons. Carlos' only expense was for his push-cart.

One reason Carlos never said much was that he spoke only in Spanish—except to give the price of a load of cartons. That he could do in English. He could also follow the main idea of a conversation in English. But to reply to a complicated matter, he preferred to speak in Spanish.

Carlos' idea at the meeting at Maxie Hammerman's was too complicated for him to explain in English. Maxie Hammerman had to explain it for him. Maxie Hammerman spoke Spanish and twelve other languages. He had to, being the Pushcart King.

"Carlos wishes to say," Maxie Hammerman began, "that the problem is to make people see who *is* blocking the streets."

"Certainly," said Harry the Hot Dog. "But how?"

"Carlos has described to me a very clever pea shooter that his youngest boy has made," said Maxie Hammerman. "Carlos says that the pea shooter shoots not just ordinary peas, but peas with a pin stuck in them."

"Children!" said Papa Peretz. "You have to watch them every minute. For example, my grandson—"

"Wait, Papa Peretz," said Maxie Hammerman, "we are coming to the point. The point is that Carlos has told his boy that he must never use such a pea shooter to shoot at people as it would not be so nice to put a pin in someone's arm."

"That's what I mean," said Papa Peretz.

"Wait," said Maxie Hammerman. "Carlos' little boy replies, 'Then what good is the shooter?' Carlos does not know how to answer, and he feels bad because the shooter is very cleverly made, and it is a shame if the boy cannot use it at all.

"Then *suddenly*," said Maxie Hammerman, "when Papa Peretz says at this meeting that we need a secret weapon, Carlos is happy. He sees what the shooter is good for."

"To put pins in the truck drivers?" said Harry the Hot Dog.

Carlos shook his head.

"No," Maxie Hammerman explained. "It is Carlos' belief that even truck drivers are people. He has told his little boy that he must never shoot at people, and he does not wish to set a bad example."

"Then what good *is* the pea shooter?" asked Frank the Flower.

Carlos spoke very excitedly to Maxie Hammerman in Spanish.

"Aha," said Maxie Hammerman. "Carlos says we will not, of course, shoot at the truck drivers. What we will shoot at is the truck tires. He says we will kill the truck tires."

"*Bang!*" said Carlos, pointing at an imaginary truck tire. "Bang, bang!" It was a word he had learned from his boy.

"Then *goma vacia!*" Carlos said.

"*Goma vacia,*" Maxie Hammerman explained, meant in Spanish 'flat tire.'

"*Si,*" Carlos nodded, blowing his breath out and sinking to the floor as if he were a truck tire going flat.

Morris the Florist took off his hat. "Such an idea!" he said. "For such an idea Carlos could be President of the U.S.A."

61

"*President!*" said Papa Peretz. "How can the President speak Spanish?"

"Never mind the President," said Harry the Hot Dog. "It is a good idea."

"*Good?*" said General Anna. "It is beautiful. I see the picture. The question is: *Who* is blocking the traffic? All right. We kill the truck tires, and suddenly everywhere in the streets —*big, dead trucks!* They can't move. They are blocking everything. People look around. In every block they see six, seven, *eight* dead trucks. People will *see* who is blocking the traffic."

"Of course," said Mr. Jerusalem, "it is not such a nice thing to do."

"Not *nice!*" said Morris the Florist. "Compared to smashing a man's cart so badly that it can never be fixed, it is a *very* nice thing to do."

"No matter how nice," said Eddie Moroney, "we should not let the truck drivers see us doing it. There could be a difference of opinion."

"Naturally," said Papa Peretz. "It should be a surprise attack. We will keep the pea shooters in our pockets. We wait until the truck driver looks the other way. Then, quick—*pffft!* Then *we* look the other way."

"Just so," said General Anna. "So it should look like an accidental flat tire."

"And all of a sudden there will be so many accidents," said Harry the Hot Dog.

"Yes," said Maxie Hammerman, figuring on a piece of

paper. "If there are five hundred and nine pushcarts, and every man who has a pushcart—"

"And every lady," said General Anna.

"And every lady," agreed Maxie Hammerman. "If every pushcart peddler kills only six tires a day, that would be quite a few accidents."

"I am all for the accidents," said Frank the Flower, "but where can we get five hundred and nine pea shooters?"

"We will make them in my shop," said Maxie Hammerman. "Carlos' boy will show us how."

"Can we also make peas?" asked Papa Peretz.

"Peas, we can grow," said Eddie Moroney. "I have a window box, and already I have grown onions and beans good enough to eat."

"Good for you, Eddie Moroney," said General Anna. "But I am not going to wait for peas to grow in your window box. Much less to dry out. We must attack at once."

"We can buy the peas," said Harry the Hot Dog.

"Yes," said Maxie Hammerman. "I will order one ton of peas in the morning."

"And a ton of pins," said General Anna.

"A ton!" said Mr. Jerusalem. "But how much will so many pins cost? Even scrap metal junk by the ton—it adds up. I should know. Scrap metal is my line. And one ton of new high-quality pins—who can afford? Not to mention one ton of peas, also an expense."

"Pin money we will need," Maxie Hammerman agreed. "And I will get it."

63

"From where?" asked Papa Peretz.

"I know a lady," said Maxie Hammerman. "She can afford to buy a few pins."

"A *few!*" said Mr. Jerusalem "One ton is a few?"

"Who is the lady?" asked General Anna.

"By the name of Wenda Gambling," said Maxie Hammerman.

"From the movies?" said Harry the Hot Dog. "You would ask *her?*"

"Why not?" said Maxie Hammerman. "In my line I have to know a lot of people. Should I be the Pushcart King for nothing?"

"And you are sure this lady will give you the money for the pins?" said Mr. Jerusalem.

"I am confident," said Maxie Hammerman, tossing his hammer in the air. "I, myself," he said, catching the hammer, "heard her say that there were too many trucks."

Maxie Hammerman was right about Wenda Gambling. She meant it about the trucks, and she was very glad to buy a ton of pins and a ton of peas as well. Not only that, but she gave Maxie Hammerman five hundred autographed pictures of herself for the pushcart peddlers to paste on their carts if they wanted to. Most of them did. Even General Anna, who did not think much of the movies, took one.

"Never mind the movies," said General Anna. "The pins, I appreciate."

CHAPTER XII

The Pea Shooter Campaign—Phase I

It took a week for the pushcart peddlers to prepare for their attack. Maxie Hammerman kept his shop open twenty-four hours a day, and the peddlers in teams of twenty men took turns putting the pins in peas.

Carlos made all five hundred and nine shooters himself. He cut them from a roll of yellow plastic tubing that a storekeeper had given him for taking away his cartons for ten years at no charge.

At last, everything was ready. The attack was set for the morning of March 23rd. The evening before, the peddlers all reported to Maxie Hammerman's shop to collect their shooters and twenty-four rounds of ammunition each.

General Anna outlined the plan of battle. Everyone was to go to the location where he usually did business. He was to wait there until 10:00 A.M., when the morning traffic would be well under way. At 10:00 sharp, he was to fire at the tires of any trucks that came in range.

Frank the Flower had wanted Wanda Gambling to fire the opening shot from in front of the Empire State Building, but General Anna felt that this would attract too much attention.

"Where there is a movie star," said General Anna, "There is a crowd. We do not want the trucks to know what is hitting them."

So the Pea Shooter Campaign began in quite an ordinary way. Between 10:05 A.M. and 10:10 A.M. on March 23rd, ninety-seven truck drivers in different parts of the city discovered that they had flat tires. Not one of the drivers knew what had hit him.

Ninety-seven hits (out of some five hundred pea-pins that were fired in the opening attack) is, according to the Amateur Weapons Association, a very good average, especially as many of the peddlers had never handled a pea shooter before. And there were a few, like Mr. Jerusalem, who had grave doubts about the whole idea.

Mr. Jerusalem's heart was not in the attack. Though he had voted with the other peddlers to fight the trucks, fighting of any sort went against his nature. Mr. Jerusalem's performance on the first morning of the Pea Shooter Campaign is, therefore, of special interest.

At the time of the Pushcart War, Mr. Jerusalem was already an old man. No one knew exactly how old. He was held in great respect by the other pushcart peddlers, because his cart was not only his business, but it was also his home.

Unlike the other peddlers, Mr. Jerusalem did not have a room where he went to sleep or cook his meals. Instead he had a small frying pan, a cup, and a tin plate which he hung neatly from the underside of his cart. He had a charcoal burner built into one corner of the cart so that he could cook for himself whenever he felt like a hot meal.

Mr. Jerusalem's favorite joke was: "Some people go out to dinner on special occasions. I eat out all the time." This was true. Mr. Jerusalem was often to be seen sitting on a curb eating a plate of beans or turnips that he had cooked himself.

At night Mr. Jerusalem dropped canvas sheets over the sides of his cart so that there was a sort of tent underneath the cart. Then he would park the cart under a tree or in a vacant lot, crawl under the cart, roll up in a quilt, and go to sleep. In the summer he often did not bother with the canvas sheets, but slept alongside the cart so that he could see the stars. He was usually the first peddler on the streets in the morning.

Mr. Jerusalem had lived this way for fifty or sixty years,

and he had never picked a fight with anyone. His motto was: "I live the way I want. You don't bother me. And I won't bother you."

Having lived by this motto for so long, Mr. Jerusalem was not happy about the Pea Shooter Campaign. To be sure, he had a great deal more at stake than the other peddlers. In his case, it was not only his business, but his home that was in danger as long as the trucks continued to attack the pushcarts. Still it went against his deepest convictions to cause another man trouble.

"There are not troubles enough in the world?" he had asked

himself as he had worked alongside the other peddlers, putting pins in the peas. "Why should I make more?"

Mr. Jerusalem was still asking himself this question as he set off down Delancey Street on the morning of March 23rd. Like the other peddlers, Mr. Jerusalem was fully armed, although no one walking down the street would have noticed.

Anyone glancing at Mr. Jerusalem would have taken the yellow plastic straw sticking from his coat pocket for a yellow pencil. And no one would have taken any notice at all of the two dozen peas with a pin stuck carefully through the center of each, which Mr. Jerusalem had pinned to the sleeve of his jacket.

Or, even if someone had noticed, he would have supposed that Mr. Jerusalem had twenty-four tiny sleeve buttons on his jacket. Mr. Jerusalem's clothes never looked like anyone else's anyway. He picked them up here and there, secondhand, and he had his own style of wearing them.

"A sleeveful of ammunition!" Mr. Jerusalem muttered to himself, as he set off on the morning of March 23rd to pick up a secondhand popcorn machine that he had arranged to buy. "Who would believe it?

"A man my age—going to war!" Mr. Jerusalem shook his head sadly. "I can hardly believe it myself.

"Fighting in the streets!" he continued. "A man of peace for eighty years is walking fully armed down Delancey Street. A man who does not care for fighting.

"It is not only that I do not care for fighting," he went on.

69

"Naturally, I do not care for fighting," he admitted. "But it is also that fighting a ten-ton truck with a pea shooter is a little crazy. I do not think it will work.

"But what else can we do?" he asked himself.

He could not think of anything else. "So I will fight," he said. "If I have to," he added.

All the same Mr. Jerusalem was relieved when at 10:00 o'clock, the hour the attack was to begin, there was no truck parked within a hundred feet of his cart. Mr. Jerusalem did not think he could hit the tire of a moving truck.

"Would General Anna want me to waste the ammunition?" he asked himself. "Or Maxie Hammerman? Or Miss Wenda Gambling who has been so kind as to pay for one ton of pins? Not to mention peas."

When Mr. Jerusalem arrived at the candy store where he was to pick up the popcorn machine, he parked his cart. He was just starting into the store, when someone shouted at him.

Mr. Jerusalem looked around and saw a Leaping Lema. The driver of the Leaping Lema was trying to back into a space in front of Mr. Jerusalem's cart. The truck was loaded with new glass-and-chromium popcorn machines.

Now if there was any kind of truck that Mr. Jerusalem did not like, it was a Leaping Lema. The reason for this was that Mr. Jerusalem had known Louie Livergreen's father.

Louie's father had been, before his death, one of the most-respected pushcart peddlers in the secondhand-clothes line. Mr. Jerusalem had often made a cup of tea on his charcoal

70

burner for Solomon Livergreen when he and Solomon were working on the same street.

Mr. Jerusalem should have been glad that Solomon's son was a big success—people said Louie Livergreen now owned one hundred big trucks. But Mr. Jerusalem held it against Louie Livergreen that from the day Louie had got his first truck, he had never come to see his father again. So every time Mr. Jerusalem saw a Leaping Lema on the streets, he thought, "They are breaking up family life."

As he watched the Leaping Lema backing into the curb on the first day of the Pea Shooter Campaign, Mr. Jerusalem wondered what his old friend Solomon Livergreen would have thought of the Pushcart War. Would Solomon, he wondered, have shot at a truck belonging to his own son, Louie Livergreen? And what would Solomon have wished his old friend Mr. Jerusalem to do?

"Shoot if you have to." That is what Solomon Livergreen would say, Mr. Jerusalem said to himself.

Mr. Jerusalem's conversation with Solomon Livergreen was interrupted by the driver of the Leaping Lema.

"Hey, Bud," shouted the driver. "Stop talking to yourself and move the baby buggy!" The driver was Little Miltie, a driver mentioned in the diary of Joey Kafflis.

Mr. Jerusalem frowned. It was bad enough that Little Miltie, a man one half the age of Mr. Jerusalem and not as tall, should call Mr. Jerusalem "Bud." But that Little Miltie should call Mr. Jerusalem's cart, which was also his home, a "baby

71

buggy"—this was unnecessarily rude. However, Mr. Jerusalem answered courteously.

"I will only be a minute," he said.

"I can't wait a minute," said Little Miltie. "I got to deliver a popcorn machine."

"Well," said Mr. Jerusalem, "I have to pick up a popcorn machine. And until I pick up this secondhand popcorn machine, there will be no room in the store for a new machine such as you wish to deliver." And he turned to go about his business.

But as Mr. Jerusalem started into the candy store, Little Miltie raced his motor. Mr. Jerusalem hesitated. He remembered what had happened to Morris the Florist. He glanced over his shoulder.

"I'm backing up, Bud," Little Miltie said.

Mr. Jerusalem sighed and walked back to move his cart to the other side of the street.

Little Miltie grinned. "That's a good boy, Buster."

Mr. Jerusalem did not reply, but as Little Miltie was backing into the place Mr. Jerusalem had left, the old peddler took out his pea shooter. He looked at it doubtfully.

"A man my age—with a *pea shooter!*" he sighed. "Such a craziness on Delancey Street." However, he inserted one of the pea-pins, took careful aim—and fired.

For a moment nothing happened. Mr. Jerusalem felt foolish. "All right, I admit it," he said. "We are all crazy."

Mr. Jerusalem was about to drop his pea shooter in the gut-

72

ter when he heard a slight hissing sound—the sound of air escaping from a tire.

"Or perhaps not so crazy," said Mr. Jerusalem.

He put the pea shooter back in his pocket and went to collect the popcorn machine. When he came out of the candy store, one of Little Miltie's rear tires was quite flat. Little Miltie was stamping up and down in the street and speaking even more rudely to the tire than he had spoken to Mr. Jerusalem.

"What is the matter?" asked Mr. Jerusalem. "The Leaping Lema is not leaping so good? A little trouble maybe?"

But Little Miltie was too angry to reply.

"Believe me, Solomon, I had to do it," Mr. Jerusalem said, as if to his old friend Solomon Livergreen.

"The fact is, Solomon," he continued, as he roped the popcorn machine onto his cart, "to cause a little trouble now and then is maybe good for a man.

"But, Solomon," he asked as he set off down Delancey Street, "who would have thought a man of my age would be such a good shot?

"Naturally, it pays to use high-quality pins," he added.

Although Mr. Jerusalem knew where he could get a good price for the secondhand popcorn machine, he was now in no hurry to get there. He paused to look over every truck that had stopped for a traffic light or had pulled up to a curb to make a delivery.

Mr. Jerusalem chose his targets very carefully, and to his

astonishment he hit four more trucks before he ran out of ammunition. At 2:30 in the afternoon, he headed back to Maxie Hammerman's for more pea-pins. He still had not got around to selling his popcorn machine.

CHAPTER XIII

Maxie Hammerman's Battle Plan & General Anna's
Hester Street Strategy

Although Mr. Jerusalem was no more than half a mile from Maxie Hammerman's shop when he ran out of ammunition, it took him nearly three hours to get there. For by mid-afternoon, the city was a mess.

In the Delancey Street area, things were particularly bad. In every block Mr. Jerusalem saw two or three trucks stranded. Traffic was at a standstill, and people were shouting at the truck drivers for blocking the streets.

The truck drivers were furious. They were not used to

75

being honked at and shouted at, and they had no idea what was happening to them.

The first few truckers who were hit thought that they had had the bad luck to pick up a splinter of glass or a nail. They telephoned for garage mechanics to come and help them change their flats, and went to have some coffee while they waited for the mechanics.

The truck drivers did not realize that their troubles were anything out of the ordinary until the mechanics began to sound irritated with them. Around noon, the mechanics began to snap at the truck drivers who called for emergency service.

"Hold your horses, Buddy," more than one driver was told. "I got fourteen flats ahead of you, and you'll just have to wait until tomorrow." At that point, the truck drivers began to wonder.

Most of the stalled trucks were so big that a truck driver by himself could not possibly change a tire. So a driver had little choice but to sit with his truck and wait for help, getting crosser and crosser as the day wore on.

Mr. Jerusalem was impressed that the afternoon papers were already warning motorists that Delancey Street was a "disaster area" and that there were terrible tie-ups in other parts of the city. It was 5:30 before Mr. Jerusalem could get his cart through the tangled traffic to Maxie Hammerman's shop. In many streets, pushcarts were the only vehicles that were getting through at all.

By the time Mr. Jerusalem did get to Maxie's, Maxie had an enormous street map of New York City tacked on his wall. As the peddlers came in to report, Maxie had been sticking pea-pins in the streets where truck tires had been hit. These pea-pins had been painted a bright red, so that one could see at a glance how the battle was going.

There were a few gold pea-pins scattered among the red. Maxie explained that these were for the really big hits—such as trailer trucks or Mighty Mammoths or Ten-Ton Tigers.

"Or Leaping Lemas?" asked Mr. Jerusalem.

"If you got a Lema, I'll give you gold," said Maxie.

The map was already peppered with red and gold pea-pins. Mr. Jerusalem studied the map with pleasure. The battle looked very neat and well-organized on Maxie's map.

"On the streets," said Mr. Jerusalem, "it does not look so neat."

"That I know," said Maxie Hammerman as he stuck five pea-pins into the map for Mr. Jerusalem—four red and one gold. Although Maxie had not left his shop all day, he had the clearest picture of the battle because all the peddlers had been coming in to report to him.

"If there is, by chance, a street where the trucks have been getting through," said Maxie, "I can see it on the map. So whenever someone comes back to the shop for ammunition, I can advise him where it is most needed."

"So far, Harry the Hot Dog has the record," Maxie told Mr. Jerusalem. "He has killed twenty-three tires, and he has come in for ammunition twice."

"How wonderful to be young," said Mr. Jerusalem. "We should give him a medal."

"We will," said Maxie Hammerman. "The only thing that is worrying me," he added, "is General Anna."

"She has not been caught?" said Mr. Jerusalem.

"No, she has not been caught," Maxie said. "Though I do not know why. She cannot aim at all."

"It is hard for a lady," said Mr. Jerusalem.

"She comes to me in tears at twelve o'clock noon," Maxie said, "to tell me she has shot twenty-five pea-pins and has not hit one tire."

"Hitting is not important," said Mr. Jerusalem. "It is the spirit."

"I tried to tell her," said Maxie Hammerman. "But General

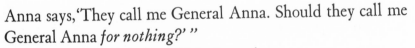

Anna says, 'They call me General Anna. Should they call me General Anna *for nothing?*' "

"It does not matter," said Mr. Jerusalem.

"Oho," said Maxie. "To General Anna, it matters. So, do you know what she is doing now?"

"What?" said Mr. Jerusalem.

"She is sticking in the pea-pins by hand," Maxie said.

"By *hand!*" said Mr. Jerusalem. "But anyone could see her do it."

"I told her," said Maxie Hammerman. "I told her—'In broad daylight you are creeping up to a truck that is parked to deliver pajama trimmings on Hester Street! Are you crazy?'

"I tell her," Maxie explained, "that this is much too dangerous. Do you know what she says?"

81

"What?" said Mr. Jerusalem.

"She says, 'Don't worry. Who would suspect an old lady of putting a pea-pin in a tire? If anyone asks me why I am bending over in the street, I tell them that I am looking for a hat pin that I have dropped under the truck.'"

Mr. Jerusalem groaned. "We shouldn't let her do it."

"She has even had a policeman helping her look for a hat pin," said Maxie Hammerman.

"We must stop her," said Mr. Jerusalem.

"But she has killed fourteen tires," said Maxie Hammerman. "Since twelve o'clock noon."

"By *hand?*" said Mr. Jerusalem.

ISED TRUCK
TIRES

CHAPTER XIV

Some Theories As to the Cause of the Flat Tires:
The Rotten-Rubber Theory, The Scattered-Pea-Tack Theory,
and The Enemy-from-Outer-Space Theory

As the pushcart peddlers had hoped, the truck drivers had no idea what had hit them. There were clearly too many casualties in those first days of the Pea Shooter Campaign to be laid to bad luck. But the truckers did not know who to blame.

Big Moe, at first, blamed the tire company he traded with. He accused the firm of putting rotten rubber in their tires.

Big Moe's suggestion so offended the president of the tire

company that he refused to sell Big Moe any more tires. This turned out to be very inconvenient. Big Moe was suddenly very much in need of extra tires, and other tire companies were so busy filling orders for their regular customers that they could not spare any tires for Big Moe.

It was curious, but for three days no one who changed a truck tire found the pea-pin that had done the damage. Either the pea-pins had worked themselves down between the deep grooves of the tires, or the pea had been broken off by the weight of the tire. It sometimes took five to ten minutes for the air to escape from a punctured tire. So drivers whose trucks were hit while moving often did not discover the damage until they stopped for a light half a mile from where they'd been hit.

Even those few mechanics who found pins in tires did not think them any odder at first than the nails or screws or bits of glass that they were always removing from tires. Finally, one sharp-eyed mechanic found a whole undamaged pea-pin, and when he extracted two more the same day, he began to be suspicious.

Once the mechanics knew what to look for, they pulled quite a few pea-pins from the truck tires. No one knew what the pea-pins were, of course, because no one had ever seen one before. The newspapers printed an enlarged drawing of one. They called it a "pea-tack."

It was supposed at first that a lot of pea-tacks had somehow been scattered through the city streets, possibly by a trucker hauling a load of pea-tacks. The police checked the "P" pages of the classified section of the telephone directory, but they could find no one in the pea-tack business.

Had the police looked under "Peas, Dried," they would have found Posey's Pea Co. ("By the Ounce, By the Pound, By the Ton"). And Mr. Posey might have told them that a lady named Wenda Gambling had ordered one ton of peas ten days before, and the police might have looked into that.

As it was, the police did not think of questioning Mr. Posey, and Mr. Posey did not think of telling the police about Wenda Gambling's order, because he did not make any connection between his peas and the pea-tacks the newspapers were talking about, as the peas he sold had no tacks in them.

On orders from Mayor Emmett P. Cudd ("Big Trucks Mean Progress"), the Police Commissioner sent out several patrols to sweep the streets, hoping to clean up the pea-tacks. The patrols found a few pea-pins that had missed their mark, but not enough to make it worth their while.

At the height of the mystery, a truck driver named Mack —the same Mack who had run down Morris the Florist— developed a theory that the pea-tacks were coming from

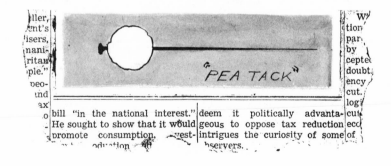

Outer Space. An invisible enemy, Mack suggested, was circling the earth and spitefully bombarding it with pea-tacks. The fact that no one had ever seen a pea-tack before and that there were no pea-tacks listed in the New York telephone book gave some weight to the Outer Space Theory.

Mack's theory resulted in a number of truckers driving about the city with their heads out the window of their cabs. There was a rash of head-on collisions of trucks whose drivers were scanning the sky for pea-tacks.

The Outer Space Theory was the most frightening theory so far proposed, as it suggested the additional possibility that the pea-tacks might be radioactive. Tests, of course, were run on the pea-tacks that the mechanics had collected. None of these showed any radioactivity, and this calmed the general public, but the truck drivers remained uneasy.

Mack pointed out that the tests had been run on only a few pea-tacks, and that there was no proof at all that other pea-tacks might not be contaminated. Or, as a friend of Mack's suggested, that the radioactivity had not passed from the pea-tacks into the tires.

At this point, the morale of the truck drivers was very low, and many talked of quitting and going into some other line of work. The truck companies did everything they could to reassure their drivers. Several of the companies hired pea-tack spotters to ride on the hoods of the trucks.

The spotters were supposed to scan the skies and signal the drivers if they saw any pea-tacks in the air. Although the spotters signaled the drivers at frequent intervals, the signals

all proved to be false alarms over a stray butterfly, or a scrap of paper that someone had dropped from an office window. No one ever produced a pea-tack that had come from Outer Space.

Finally it occurred to a newspaper reporter to ask Mack how he explained the fact that it was only *truck* tires that were getting hit. This was the first intelligent thinking that there had been on the problem, and it might have led to something had not a lady called a newspaper to say that it wasn't *true* that only truck tires were getting hit. She said that she had been painfully pricked by a pea-tack as she was crossing Second Avenue.

"Who missed?" demanded Maxie Hammerman when the newspapers reported this interesting development.

"I didn't miss," said Harry the Hot Dog. "She insulted my sauerkraut, and for once I couldn't resist."

"For once we understand," said General Anna. "But it shouldn't happen twice."

General Anna had to be firm with Harry the Hot Dog, as he was such a good shot that his friends were now calling him Harry the Hot Shot, which he did not mind at all. In fact, he was so pleased with himself that he would not have hesitated to shoot at Mayor Emmett P. Cudd himself, if anyone had dared him to.

"I am warning you, Harry the Hot Dog," said General Anna. "We are not shooting innocent people. That will only make trouble."

What most infuriated the truck drivers was that no one seemed to feel sorry for them. People would call out to a stalled driver, "What's the matter, Mister? A little trouble?" But they would smile as they asked the question, and no one ever offered to help a driver change a tire.

The truth was that it seemed to amuse people to see an enormous truck made helpless by a mere flat tire. Newspaper cartoonists kept drawing humorous pictures of the handicapped trucks, and one television comedian made himself famous overnight by his imitation of a truck in trouble.

Of course, there was great inconvenience to the city with trucks stalled everywhere. But the trucks had been inconveniencing the city for a long time, and the fact that the trucks themselves were the most inconvenienced by this new development seemed to cheer people, and they did not complain too much.

When the breakdowns began, the truck drivers had simply left their trucks in the middle of the streets until they could get mechanics to help them change the flat tires. But by the fourth day of the Pea Shooter Campaign, there were so many trucks disabled that the Traffic Commissioner issued an emergency order requiring that all vehicles with flat tires must be removed from the streets within one hour of the time the flat was reported. The penalty for leaving a truck in the middle of the street was $500.

As there were not enough tow trucks in the city to get all the stalled trucks off the streets, the truckers whose tires had not been hit had to stop their regular delivery work to tow their friends to garages. And from time to time one saw tow trucks with flat tires being towed by regular trucks.

When a truck carrying perishable goods—fruit or vegetables—broke down, the driver often had to hire half a dozen pushcarts to unload the truck and deliver the goods before they spoiled. This was very good business for the pushcarts.

"With the extra work," said Eddie Moroney, "we can—if necessary—buy more pins."

By the sixth day of the Pea Shooter Campaign, the number of trucks in the streets was reduced enough so that the traffic flowed at a brisk pace for the first time in ten years. There were occasional tie-ups caused by the pushcart peddlers shooting down more trucks, but the trucks were removed in a short time.

CHAPTER XV

The Arrest of Frank the Flower

On the ninth day of the Pea Shooter Campaign, Frank the Flower was arrested. A pea-tack spotter spotted him.

A few of the trucking companies had become dissatisfied with Mack's theory about the pea-tacks coming from Outer Space. These companies had removed their pea-tack spotters from the hoods of their trucks and stationed them on the tailgates of the trucks—or on the rear bumpers—with orders to watch for an enemy on the ground.

One of these spotters, riding on the tailgate of a moving van, saw Frank the Flower aiming at one of the rear tires of the van. At first he thought Frank was just moistening the tip of a yellow pencil. But when the van slowed down for a red light a few blocks later, the spotter heard air escaping from one of the truck's rear tires, and he remembered the look of concentration on Frank the Flower's face as he had put the "pencil" to his mouth.

While the driver got out to examine his punctured tire, the spotter ran back three blocks and was just in time to catch Frank the Flower sighting at another truck. The spotter did not actually see the pea-pin leave the shooter, but when the truck Frank the Flower had been aiming at limped to the curb with a flat tire before it reached the next corner, the spotter called a policeman and demanded that he search Frank the Flower.

When the policeman found the shooter in Frank the Flower's pocket and asked what it was, Frank said that it was a yellow plastic straw made for him by a good friend.

"In case I should order a bottle of cream soda and the restaurant should be out of straws," Frank explained.

"Cream soda?" said the policeman. He looked a little doubtful.

"My favorite drink," said Frank. "Some people don't mind drinking from a bottle," he added. "But I prefer to have a straw."

"My wife is like that," said the policeman, and he was about to give the shooter back to Frank the Flower when his eye fell on the half dozen pea-pins that Frank the Flower had stuck in his hatband.

Frank the Flower was about to suggest that they were imitation-pearl corsage pins that he gave out with special orders—in case a lady wanted to pin a bunch of flowers on her dress. But the spotter had already recognized them as the peatacks that the truckers had been finding in their tires.

Frank the Flower had no choice but to confess to shooting down the two trucks the spotter claimed he had shot down, especially after the spotter succeeded in finding the pea-pins in the tires.

The question arose then as to how many other trucks Frank the Flower might have shot down. Frank said he would have to think.

This was a difficult question for Frank. He had shot down either seventeen or eighteen trucks. But he could not be sure which.

On the second day of the Pea Shooter Campaign, one truck that was running through a red light had got away before Frank could tell whether he had scored a flat. And this one truck had been confusing his count ever since.

Some days Frank felt it was perfectly fair to count it. Other days he had to admit that he would be giving himself the benefit of the doubt.

Quite probably it *was* eighteen, he told himself, as the policeman waited for his answer. And while eighteen was not in the class with Harry the Hot Dog, it sounded suddenly like a very high score. Although Frank felt a certain pride in the matter, he did not want to be in any more trouble with the police than necessary. In which case, it would be better to say seventeen.

Frank considered the matter all the way to the police station. At the police station, the Police Commissioner himself took charge of the questioning.

"All right," said the Police Commissioner, when the officer who had arrested Frank had explained the problem. "How many?"

Frank the Flower wondered how long he would have to stay in jail if he did confess to eighteen.

"I'm waiting," said the Police Commissioner.

"Well," said Frank cautiously, "at least seventeen."

"At *least*," said the Police Commissioner. "And at most?"

"Maybe eighteen," Frank said uncertainly.

"*Maybe?*" said the Police Commissioner. "Now see here. There have been 18,991 flat tires reported in the last week, and I intend to find out who shot down every one of them. So how many *did* you shoot down? At most?"

It was at this moment that Frank the Flower became a hero. He looked the Police Commissioner in the eye. "Okay, I admit it," he said. "I shot them all."

"*All* of them!" said the Police Commissioner.

"All eighteen," Frank said. "All eighteen thousand, that is. I count by thousands."

"Eighteen *thousand!*" gasped the Police Commissioner.

Frank smiled apologetically. "Maybe a few more or less. I lose track."

94

"But eighteen thousand—" said the astonished Commissioner.

"All of them," Frank said firmly. "I shot them all."

"*All* 18,991!" said the Police Commissioner.

Frank the Flower nodded. When the Police Commissioner mentioned the large number of flat tires that had been reported, Frank suddenly realized that if he confessed to shooting down only seventeen or eighteen, the police would go on looking for whoever had shot down the rest. If that happened, all his friends might be arrested, too, and that would be the end of the Pea Shooter Campaign.

Frank decided that as long as he had already been arrested,

he might as well take the blame for everything. It was better, he reasoned, that the police had caught him than Harry the Hot Dog, who was a better aim. Not that eighteen was anything to be ashamed of.

"*All* 18,991?" asked the Police Commissioner as if he had not heard correctly the first time.

"I lose track of the exact number," said Frank the Flower. Maxie Hammerman's map at last count had had over 20,000 pea-pins in it, but Frank the Flower did not like to tell the Police Commissioner that his count was off by a thousand or more. He felt sure that would annoy the Police Commissioner.

"I cannot be sure down to the last tire," said Frank the Flower. "But I have been at it several days now."

The Police Commissioner could hardly believe his luck in having got a full confession so easily. The truck drivers had been giving him a great deal of trouble with their complaints, and he was tired of the whole affair.

"But what did you do it for?" asked the Police Commission. "Have you got something against the trucks?"

Frank the Flower shrugged. "I am a crackpot," he said.

"I *thought* so," said the Police Commissioner. Being a sensible man himself, he took the view that only a crackpot could have done what Frank the Flower had confessed to doing.

Besides, Frank the Flower did not look to the Police Commissioner like a criminal type. This was mainly because of the hat Frank wore. It was an old felt hat with the crown cut out of it and small flowers of different colors—mostly bachelor buttons and jonquils—tucked in the hatband. (Frank the Flower put fresh flowers in the hatband every morning.)

Frank the Flower's hat was not really such an odd hat for someone in the flower line to wear. In a way, it was a kind of advertisement. However, the Police Commissioner had never seen a hat like this before.

The Police Commissioner felt that it definitely was *not* the kind of hat a true criminal type would wear. But he thought it might very well be the sort of hat that a crackpot would wear.

"But *18,991* tires!" said the Police Commissioner.

"It was nothing," said Frank the Flower modestly.

The Police Commissioner sat studying Frank the Flower for several minutes. Then he called the policeman who had arrested Frank. "You will have to lock this man up," he said. "But treat him gently. He is a harmless crackpot."

The Police Commissioner patted Frank kindly on the shoulder. He was much relieved to have solved the pea-tack problem.

Within half an hour, extras, announcing the arrest of Frank the Flower, were on the newsstands. "SPOTTER SPOTS PEA-TACKER," said one headline. "PEA-TACKER CAP-TURED," said another. "TACK-MAN IS CRACKPOT," said a third. Under the headlines there were pictures of Frank the Flower.

When General Anna saw the headlines, she sent out word that all peddlers should report at once to Maxie Hammerman's. In the cellar of Maxie Hammerman's shop, the peddlers listened to the Police Commissioner on the radio.

The Police Commissioner was assuring the public that there was no further cause for alarm. The mystery of the punctured truck tires had been solved, he said. It had all been the work of a harmless crackpot.

The Police Commissioner's announcement brought tears to the eyes of some of Frank's friends, They realized that he was trying to protect them by taking all the blame himself.

"For such an idea, he should be President of the U.S.A.," said Morris the Florist.

"*President!*" said Papa Peretz. "How can the President be a crackpot? Not that I do not appreciate what Frank the Flower has done," he added.

"He is a hero," said General Anna. "May he live a hundred years."

"A hundred years?" said Mr. Jerusalem. "So he can spend them all in jail maybe. For so many truck tires, Frank the Flower could stay in jail for the rest of his life."

Mr. Jerusalem, who was used to sleeping under the stars, could not think of anything worse than being shut in a jail cell. He did not think it was right that Frank the Flower should take all the blame.

"We must all take our share," he said. "We must go to the Police Commissioner and explain."

"No," said General Anna. "If we all confess, the war is

98

finished, and it is the trucks who have won. By taking the blame, Frank the Flower is telling us that he wishes us to carry on. How can we let him down when he is in so much trouble to help us?"

"No, we cannot let him down," said Harry the Hot Dog. "I, personally, will kill ten tires for Frank the Flower this afternoon."

"Wait," said Eddie Moroney. "As long as Frank the Flower is in jail, we cannot kill any more tires."

"Why not?" said Harry the Hot Dog. "You do not agree with General Anna that we must carry on?"

"I always agree with General Anna," said Eddie Moroney. "Of course, we must win the war. I am only pointing out that if there are any more flat tires, the Police Commissioner will not believe Frank the Flower's story that he himself has killed all those trucks. The police will look again. And now that they know what to look for, how long do you think it will be before they are arresting every pushcart peddler in the city?"

"Eddie Moroney is right," said General Anna. "Everybody will turn in his shooter and ammunition before leaving Maxie Hammerman's shop tonight."

"Everyone?" said Harry the Hot Dog. Harry the Hot Dog had had more fun shooting at truck tires than he had ever had before. He was proud of holding the record for the most tires killed, and he was even a little jealous that Frank the Flower (who had killed only seventeen or eighteen tires) should be getting *all* the credit in the newspapers.

"It is not the end of the war," said General Anna. "It is only the end of the Pea Shooter Campaign. We must find a new weapon."

CHAPTER XVI

Big Moe's Attack on the Police Commissioner

It was fortunate that General Anna had called in all the pea shooters on the day of Frank the Flower's arrest. For the day after Frank's arrest, the newspaper headlines read: "BIG MOE CALLS POLICE COMMISSIONER BIG DOPE."

Big Moe said that the Police Commissioner was a fool to believe Frank the Flower's story. Big Moe pointed out that it was impossible for Frank the Flower to have been in all the places where the trucks had been shot down—even if he was a crackpot.

Big Moe gave as proof the fact that two Mammoth Moving trucks had been shot down on the first morning of the Pea Shooter Campaign. One of these trucks was shot down at 10:05 A.M. on 179th Street, and the other at 10:07 A.M. on 2nd Street.

"How could any man travel 177 blocks in two minutes?" Big Moe asked. "Especially in New York City traffic," he added.

Big Moe claimed that there was obviously a widespread conspiracy. He demanded that the Police Commissioner appoint a special Pea-Tack Squad to search for other "pea-tackers."

As setting up a Pea-Tack Squad would be admitting that he *had* been a big dope to believe Frank the Flower, the Police Commissioner told Big Moe to go sit on a pea-tack.

Big Moe did not take the Police Commissioner's advice. Instead, he called Mayor Emmett P. Cudd.

Mayor Emmett P. Cudd was very concerned about the trouble the trucks were having. After Mayor Cudd's famous Peanut Butter Speech, Big Moe had made the Mayor a present of 1,000 shares of stock in the Mammoth Moving Company as a token of appreciation of all Mayor Cudd was doing for big business.

The Tiger and Louis Livergreen naturally had not wished to be outdone by Big Moe. So they, too, had given Mayor Cudd tokens of their appreciation in the form of 1,000 shares in Tiger Trucking and the same number of shares in LEMA.

With all these tokens, the Mayor could not help having a real interest in the trucking business. As a result, Mayor Cudd and The Three were on the friendliest of terms. They played cards together every Friday night, and the Mayor was kept well informed about trucking problems.

"Your problems are my problems," he frequently said to The Three.

Therefore, when Big Moe called the Mayor to say, "Speaking as a friend, I think you ought to have the Police Commissioner appoint a Pea-Tack Squad to get to the bottom of this conspiracy," the Mayor took it as a friendly suggestion. He passed it on to the Police Commissioner.

102

The Police Commissioner did not take it as a friendly suggestion, but he had no choice. He organized a Pea-Tack Squad and ordered the Squad to comb the city for pea-tacks or pea-tackers.

However, thanks to General Anna's orders, there was nothing for the Squad to find. All the ammunition was locked in Maxie Hammerman's basement, and no trucks were shot down for three days.

"Well," people said, "never underestimate the power of a crackpot!"

There was even a little disappointment among the general public that the excitement was over. The mysterious attack on the trucks had become a popular topic of conversation, and there had been a good deal of friendly betting on the daily tire casualties.

There were two theories to account for the 177 blocks that so disturbed Big Moe. One was that Frank the Flower had had a heliocopter. The second, and more widely-held explanation, was that Frank *had* shot down the truck on 2nd Street, but that the flat on 179th Street was caused by an ordinary nail.

The failure of the Pea-Tack Squad to find a widespread conspiracy made Big Moe look foolish, which cheered the Police Commissioner. The headlines now read: "POLICE COMMISSIONER SAYS BIG MOE HAS BIG IMAGINATION."

"I always thought Frank the Flower was an honest man,"

the Police Commissioner told reporters. "I can usually spot a crackpot when I see one."

But the Police Commissioner had cheered up a little too soon. The day after he spoke his mind, new outbreaks of flat tires were reported. The reports came from three different sections of the city.

CHAPTER XVII

The Pea Shooter Campaign—Phase II

The pushcart peddlers were as surprised as the Police Commissioner by the reports of new attacks on the trucks. General Anna summoned everyone to Maxie Hammerman's to find out whether any peddlers had not turned in their pea shooters as ordered.

Everyone had. Even Harry the Hot Dog, whom General Anna questioned privately, gave General Anna his word that —much as he had hated to do it—he had turned in his shooter and every pea-pin in his possession.

The mystery was solved when the Pea-Tack Squad caught

several boys between the ages of eight and ten shooting down trucks near Manhattan Bridge. The boys were using shooters very much like Frank the Flower's and the police demanded to know where they had got them and whether they knew Frank the Flower.

The children said that they had never met Frank the Flower and that they had made the shooters themselves from the description of Frank the Flower's shooter in the newspapers. One of the boys had even made himself a hat like Frank the Flower's, though the flowers stuck in the hatband were made of paper.

The Pea-Tack Squad confiscated the shooters from the children and asked them to please not make any more. But by that time other children had had the same idea, and there were soon children all over the city making shooters and shooting at truck tires. Frank-the-Flower Clubs sprang up in several neighborhoods.

The Pea-Tack Squad no sooner caught one gang of children than they received a call about another. And since there were in the city many more children between the ages of eight and ten than there were pushcart peddlers, there were at the height of the children's campaign even more flat tires than there had been before Frank the Flower's arrest.

One day Big Moe reported that 36 out of his 72 trucks were laid up. The whole thing was a scandal, he said.

"Any minute," he warned, "these hoodlums will start shooting innocent people. Then perhaps the Police Commissioner will do something."

Curiously, the children never did start shooting at people —or cars—or taxis—or bicycles. There seemed to be a clear understanding among the children that this was a war against the trucks, and that it was more fun to keep it that way.

During this phase of the Pea Shooter Campaign, all of the Five & Ten's in the city did a brisk business in tacks and pins. (The children found that both worked equally well.) Grocery stores had a great many calls for dried peas, and florists reported a surprising increase in business from customers between the ages of eight and ten. Morris the Florist began making up small bunches of day-old flowers suitable for hatbands and selling them at a special low price to anyone under the age of ten.

It was natural that the truck drivers should have been unnerved by Phase One of the Pea Shooter Campaign, when they did not know who was shooting at them. However, they were even more unnerved by Phase Two, after it had been established that it was children who were doing the shooting.

As there were children all over the city, the truck drivers did not feel safe anywhere. If there was a child anywhere in sight, a truck driver hesitated to leave his truck to make a delivery or to have a cup of coffee. Most drivers thought twice about driving down a block where they could see children at play.

Although only a small number of the children in the city were involved in the shooting, it was almost impossible to judge from appearance alone which children might have pea shooters concealed in their jackets. One driver's suspicions got so out of hand that he had his own children searched for pea shooters every night before dinner.

When the children realized that the truck drivers were afraid of them, it was hard for them to resist teasing the drivers. Even those children so strictly brought up that they would not have thought of shooting at a truck tire, much less joining a Frank-the-Flower Club, got a good deal of satisfaction out of just hanging around parked trucks. Two or three children had only to stand on the sidewalk near a truck to give a truck driver the jitters.

"Don't trust *any* of them," Big Moe instructed his drivers. "If a kid gets within a hundred feet of your truck, clobber him." Clobbering, unfortunately, made enemies of even friendly, reliable children.

Matters went from bad to worse. Truckers, driving through blocks where children were playing, panicked and stepped on the gas and as a result were often arrested for speeding. When policemen halted a truck to write out a speeding ticket, the truck was what Frank-the-Flower fans called a "Sitting Truck," an easy shot. The truck drivers couldn't win.

The Frank-the-Flower Clubs had a whole language of their own. The expression, "Don't be a truck" replaced, among Frank-the-Flower fans, such earlier slang as "Don't be a dope, a jerk, a square." Although "Don't be a truck" is an expression that we all use today, it dates back to Phase Two of the Pea Shooter Campaign.

"You're a crackpot," as an expression of affection also originated with the Frank-the-Flower fans, who used the phrase to mean "You're a good guy, a prince, a buddy, a doll, a sweetheart." The use of this expression undoubtedly inspired the popular polka tune of the period, "Be My Little Crackpot."

The motto of the Frank-the-Flower Clubs was: "A Frank-the-Flower man is Respectful to Police Commissioners, Automobiles, Taxis, and Older People, and Death on Trucks. A Frank-the-Flower man is Loyal, Clean, and a Good Shot."

Members of the clubs greeted each other in a kind of code. "Hi ya, Bachelor" was a popular greeting. To which the proper reply was: "Hi ya, Button." Or, "Hi ya, Rose." To which: "Hi ya, Bud," was the answer.

Each club had its own variations:

"Hi ya, Sweet." "Hi ya, Pea."

"Hi ya, Chris." "Hi ya, Anthemum."

"Hi ya, Hi ya," "Hi ya, Cinth."

"Hi ya, Daff." "Did you say *Daff?*" "I said, Hi ya, Daff."
"Oh! Hi ya, Dill."

The American Ambassador to Russia acquired a reputation
for a quick wit when a sharp-tongued Russian diplomat ad-
dressed him at a party by his first name. To the diplomat's
greeting, "Hi ya, John," the Ambassador responded without
batting an eyelash, "Hi ya, Quill"—a nickname that stuck to
the Russian for years.

The Ambassador's retort led to the President of the United
States' being asked at his next press conference whether his
Ambassador was a member of a Frank-the-Flower Club. In
defense of the Ambassador, the President simply grinned and
replied, "Don't be a truck."

This response, although it lost the President the support
of the trucking industry, greatly increased his popularity with
both automobile drivers and pedestrians. While English teachers did not approve of the President speaking in such a slangy
way, the majority of voters were impressed with the President's detailed knowledge of what was going on in every
city of the country.

The general public had mixed feelings about the children's
part in the Pushcart War. A few agreed with Big Moe
that shooting at trucks was hoodlum behavior and should
be severely punished. But the majority of people took the
attitude that children had always had pea shooters, and that
the pea-tack shooters were only a passing craze.

A respected child psychologist of the period said that in attacking the trucks, the children were expressing resentment of parents who pushed them around. "It is a classic case of the little guy against the big guy," said the psychologist. The psychologist's advice was that it was better on the whole for the children to be killing trucks than their parents. To forbid them to shoot at trucks, he suggested, might create worse problems. This made parents think twice about taking a firm stand about the trucks.

The pushcart peddlers did not know what to make of the children's campaign. It bothered Harry the Hot Dog that any eight-year-old could get away with flattening a truck while he had to stand idly by. He was much put out by a rumor that a nine-year-old boy in the East Harlem section of the city had killed almost as many trucks in one week as Harry had killed in the opening week of the Pea Shooter Campaign.

"Whose war is this, anyway?" Harry demanded.

"They are making a joke of it," he complained at a meeting that General Anna had called to discuss the situation.

"This war is a serious business," Harry said. "To pushcart peddlers, a matter of life and death. And these kids are making it like a big picnic. A big joke. They are laughing at us."

"Some joke!" said Morris the Florist. "Killing thousands of trucks. Let them joke, I say."

"Why is it a joke?" asked Papa Peretz. "Maybe they *seriously* don't like the trucks. A big truck hits a little kid. Is that a joke? I tell you, kids today are very smart."

"All those clubs!" Harry said. "They are making Frank

the Flower look silly. They are even making fun of his hat."

Maxie Hammerman laughed. "For twenty years I have made fun of Frank the Flower's hat, and he does not care. He is proud of that hat."

"Also," said Morris the Florist, "the club members are writing letters to Frank the Flower in jail, and it is nice to get letters when you are confined."

CHAPTER XVIII

The Retreat of the Trucks & Rumors of a Build-Up
on the Fashion Front

Although the children's Pea Shooter Campaign may have been, as many people said, a craze that would have died as suddenly as it had started, the truck drivers could not afford to wait and see. At the height of the children's campaign, the casualties were so heavy that the truck companies had to take their trucks off the streets.

The retreat of the trucks made it very pleasant for the people who wanted to drive around the city doing errands or a little sightseeing. It was delightful to see taxis zipping around corners again, making U-turns, and snaking in and out among the women drivers as gaily as they had in the days before the trucks had taken over the streets. Even the women drivers seemed to enjoy it. After years of battling with the trucks, dodging the taxis seemed like a game.

One sporting lady even blew a kiss to a taxi driver who clipped off her fender, and called out to him, "Well done!" (This so charmed the taxi driver, that he towed the lady to a garage, bought her a new fender, took her out to dinner, and married her.)

Indeed, everyone was in the best of spirits that first day that the trucks did not appear on the streets. It was like a holiday. The buses were loaded with ladies out shopping for new hats and perfume. Fathers took the afternoon off from their offices to take their children to the zoo. Teachers gave no homework. There were picnics in the parks, and the movie houses and bowling alleys were crowded.

All the pushcarts were back on the streets, and the pushcart peddlers did more business on that day than they had for nineteen years. The whole city was jubilant.

Except for the truck drivers, of course. The Three were quick to see that it would be dangerous to keep the trucks off the streets for more than a few days. Once people became accustomed to having the freedom of the streets again, they would object to the return of the trucks. The Three agreed that it was imperative to get the trucks back on the streets as fast as possible.

Big Moe called the Mayor and demanded that something

be done to make the streets safe for trucks. "This is very bad for business," said Big Moe. "Another week of this, and I will be out of business."

Mayor Cudd was naturally sympathetic. He summoned the City Council, and the Council proposed to put a tax on tacks sold to anyone under the age of twenty-one. It was thought that if this tax were high enough (the Council set the rate at a dollar per pound of tacks), this would discourage children from buying tacks in any quantity.

This proposal, however, was not enough to satisfy the truck drivers. What guarantee was there, they demanded, when the newspapers published the proposals, that persons *over* twenty-one might not take it into their heads to shoot at truck tires? Frank the Flower, Big Moe pointed out to Mayor Cudd, was over twenty-one.

"But he is a crackpot," said the Mayor.

"Maybe," said Big Moe. "But listen to this. My wife tells me that a very fancy store on Fifth Avenue uptown put in its window two days ago a Frank-the-Flower hat for ladies, and the price of that hat is $29.95."

"Twenty-nine, ninety-five for a crackpot hat!" said Mayor Cudd.

"That is not the point," said Big Moe. "The point is that the store *already* cannot keep up with the orders for that $29.95 hat."

"What do you mean *already?*" asked Mayor Cudd.

"I mean already before today's paper in which I see a full-page advertisement for this hat," said Big Moe.

"Look in the paper," said Big Moe. "There is a big drawing of the hat, and it says underneath: *A Real Traffic Stopper!* It also says: *Do truck drivers whistle at you? This will really flatten them!*"

"Also," said Big Moe, "I should warn you that a fashion magazine which my wife reads has on its cover this week the movie star, Wenda Gambling, in this same $29.95 Frank-the-Flower hat. And I would like to know what you will say when your wife asks you if she can have a $29.95 hat such as Wenda Gambling is wearing?"

"My wife does not ask my advice about hats," said Mayor Cudd.

"Naturally," said Big Moe. "That is the danger. Children are bad enough. But if the ladies get into this, we are finished."

The Mayor saw the danger. He called the City Council together again, and the Council amended the new tax ruling to cover the sales of tacks to persons of *all* ages.

CHAPTER XIX

The Tacks Tax & The British Ultimatum

The Tacks Tax, as all students of American history know, was the most unpopular tax in the history of New York City. It caused revolution in the city schools and almost brought England into the war.

The citizens of New York protested at once that the tax was undemocratic. They said it discriminated unfairly against the users of tacks as opposed to the users of screws, nails, bolts, and pins.

Users of screws, nails, bolts, and pins (and that took in nearly every household in the city) objected as strongly to the Tacks Tax as the tacks users. Their argument was that if the Mayor and the City Council could put a whopping tax on tacks, there was nothing to keep them from putting a whopping tax on screws, nails, bolts, and pins any time they chose.

The pushcart peddlers had no special interest in tacks, as they relied exclusively on pins for the manufacture of their ammunition. However, they supported the protest against the tax as a matter of principle.

Mr. Jerusalem risked arrest by giving away boxes of tacks to his customers, rather than charge the hated tax. He was picked up by the Pea-Tack Squad, but the Police Commissioner refused to jail him on the grounds that the Council ruling put a tax only on tacks that were *sold*. The Police Commissioner said that if Mr. Jerusalem wanted to go broke giving away tacks, that was his own business.

Teachers were among the hardest hit by the Tacks Tax, and they went on strike in protest. You could not have a bulletin board without tacks, they claimed. And you could not run a New York City classroom without a bulletin board, they said, or things got hopelessly out of hand.

Twelve thousand teachers carrying NO TACKS—NO TEACHERS signs picketed Mayor Cudd's office. And while they were picketing, the city schools had to be closed.

With the schools closed, children of school age were on the streets from morning to night, and the shooting of trucks increased accordingly. (As many of the children had been making their pea-tacks with pins all along—they couldn't see that it made any difference—the Tacks Tax did not bother them seriously.)

The strongest objection to the tax naturally came from England, who was at the time the world's largest producer of tacks. Most of the tacks used in New York City came from England.

England charged that the New York City Tacks· Tax was designed to cut England out of the American tack market and was, in fact, a violation of Section 238 of the British-American International Tack Agreement. The British Ambassador protested in the strongest of terms to the President in Washington and suggested that his country might have to intervene directly in the fighting in New York if the Tacks Tax was not at once repealed.

The President acted promptly. He called Mayor Cudd to

the White House and warned him that unless the tax law was repealed within twenty-four hours, he would have to send Federal troops to keep order in the city.

Mayor Cudd had to ask the City Council to repeal the tax he had asked them to pass the week before. The lifting of the tax was celebrated by the wildest spree of tack buying in the history of the city. (Over 800,000 pounds of tacks were sold on the first day of the repeal.) The Mayor, in alarm, hastily improvised the Pea Blockade in hopes of averting a mass outbreak of pea-shooting.

CHAPTER XX
The Pea Blockade

On the morning of May 11th, the Mayor issued an emergency order prohibiting the sale of dried peas in New York City until peace in the streets had been restored.

"No peace—no peas," said the Mayor in an address to the city, explaining the reasons for his action.

The City Council, the Mayor told the people, had contracted with Big Moe for nineteen Mighty Mammoths to blockade all bridges and tunnels leading into New York.

Mammoth drivers had been instructed to search all incoming trucks for shipments of peas.

"And furthermore," announced the Mayor, "I have ordered the Pea-Tack Squad to close all pea-packaging plants in the city until further notice."

It was the Pea Blockade and the closing of all the pea-packaging plants that led to the discovery of the Pushcart Conspiracy, although the discovery was the purest sort of accident.

All of the pea-packagers in the city objected to the shutdown order. But the Pea-Tack Squad on the whole handled matters tactfully.

The Squad pointed out to the pea-packagers that: in the first place, the pea-packagers could not get any peas to package while the Pea Blockade was in effect, and that, in the second place, they could not get any trucks to deliver their packaged peas until there was order in the streets again. Since this was true, most of the packagers—some of them grumbling a little and some of them grumbling a lot—did as they were ordered. They dismissed their workers and locked up their plants.

On the whole, the Pea Blockade went smoothly until the Pea-Tack Squad arrived at Posey's plant. Mr. P. Posey, of Posey's Peas ("By the Ounce, By the Pound, By the Ton") did not give up so easily.

Although Mr. Posey had advertised his peas "By the Ounce, By the Pound, By the Ton" for thirty-one years, he had never had an order for a ton of peas until the spring of the Pushcart

War. Most of his business was by the pound. Mr. Posey's biggest order in pre-war days had been a three-hundred-pound order from a church that was having a baked-pea barbecue.

Ever since the one-ton order, Mr. Posey had had big ideas. He was full of plans for expanding his business, and naturally he did not want to close down his plant just as his advertising was beginning to pay.

With the profits from his one-ton order, Mr. Posey had laid in a large supply of peas, enough to last through a long blockade. Moreover, he did not use trucks to deliver his packaged peas.

Mr. Posey was an old-fashioned pea merchant, and he had his peas delivered by pushcart. He had found that the pushcarts could get through the crowded streets more easily, and often faster, than the trucks. Also, their charges for delivery were less. The one-ton order had been delivered in twenty one-hundred-pound sacks by four pushcarts.

So, with a good supply of peas in his plant and no need for trucks to deliver them, Mr. Posey saw no reason at all for closing up his plant. Most of his business was with small

restaurants that featured pea soup, and he could not see that pea soup had anything to do with the war in the streets.

"This is a peaceful pea plant," Mr. Posey said to Mrs. Posey, who helped him in the business. "And nobody is going to shut us down without a fight."

CHAPTER XXI

The Barricade at Posey's Plant

When the Pea-Tack Squad arrived at Posey's plant on the second morning of the Pea Blockade, they found the doors barricaded with one-hundred-pound sacks of dried peas.

"Open up," ordered the Chief of the Pea-Tack Squad, when six Squad men could not budge the door.

"Mayor's orders," he explained, when he saw Mr. Posey glaring down at him from a second-story window of the plant.

"I'm closed today," Mr. Posey called down, "for business reasons. Tell the Mayor."

"Well, open up because I have to close you up," said the Chief.

"I'm very busy right now," said Mr. Posey.

The Pea-Tack Squad finally had to call the Fire Department. Fire engines came roaring down the street, bringing with them a large crowd.

Two firemen took an axe to Posey's door. When Mr. Posey saw the firemen chopping through his door, he and his wife began bombarding the firemen and the Pea-Tack Squad from the second floor with ten-pound sacks of dried peas.

One fireman and two Squad men were knocked unconscious and another Squad man slipped on the dried peas that were rolling all over the sidewalk and broke his wrist.

When the firemen finally broke through the door and be-

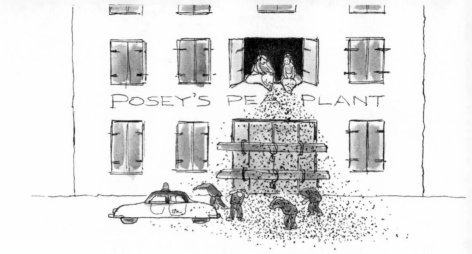

gan hacking their way through the one-hundred-pound sacks of peas Mr. Posey had stacked against it, a torrent of peas poured into the street. Hundreds of children had gathered by now, and began excitedly stuffing their pockets with peas.

By the time the Squad men had fought their way through the barricade they were pretty mad. They seized Mr. Posey and his wife and tied them up—they had to, as the Poseys kept throwing sacks of peas at them. The Chief of the Pea-Tack Squad then demanded to know why Mr. Posey had barricaded his door.

Mr. Posey, who was close to tears by now, told the truth. He said that he had closed up his place of business because he did not want the Pea-Tack Squad closing it up.

Naturally, this was too simple an explanation to satisfy the Chief of the Pea-Tack Squad. "You manufacturing something illegal in here maybe?" he asked Mr. Posey. "Counterfeit money? Dynamite?"

"*Dynamite!*" said Mr. Posey scornfully. "If I had dynamite, would I be wasting perfectly good sacks of peas, throwing them from a second-story window?

"This is a one-hundred-percent-legal pea-packaging plant," said Mr. Posey, "and all I have in this place is peas and five, ten, twenty-five, and one-hundred-pound sacks for packaging them. If you untie me, I will show you what kind of business I run."

"We'll see for ourselves," said the Chief of the Pea-Tack Squad, and he ordered two of his men to search Mr. Posey's plant.

The Squad men searched the plant from top to bottom, and they did not find anything but peas in five, ten, twenty-five, and one-hundred-pound sacks. One of the men suggested to the Chief that the sacks of peas might be a hiding place for something else, such as smuggled diamonds.

"*Diamonds!*" said Mrs. Posey. "You think we are throwing diamonds out a second-story window? It's bad enough we should waste so many peas."

The Chief, however, took out a jacknife and ripped open a dozen one-hundred-pound sacks of peas. Dried peas cascaded all over the room, and the Pea-Tack Squad found itself up to its ankles in peas.

The Chief ordered the Squad to sift through the peas to make sure that there were no packets of diamonds or pearls or gold nuggets or maybe uranium concealed among the peas. The Squad man who had suggested the diamonds wished he had kept still.

When his men found nothing, the Chief only grew more

suspicious. He asked to have Mr. Posey's business records brought to him.

It was only after the Chief had leafed carefully through Mr. Posey's books, which dated back thirty-one years, that the Chief began to feel a little ashamed. The books showed clearly that the only product Mr. Posey had sold during his long business career was dried peas.

Most of the orders, the Chief saw, were for ten and twenty-five-pound sacks. He realized then that Mr. Posey had to work very hard at his small business to make a living and that he had made a wreck of Mr. Posey's place of business for nothing.

The Chief was about to close the order books and to apologize to Mr. Posey for causing him so much trouble, when his eye fell on Wenda Gambling's order for one ton of peas. The Chief only noticed the entry because it was for such a large number of peas, as compared with Mr. Posey's usual orders.

"Not Wenda Gambling, *the movie star?*" said the Chief.

"Why not?" said Mrs. Posey. "Posey's Peas are a quality product."

"But what does a movie star want with a ton of peas?" asked the Chief.

"How do I know?" said Mr. Posey. "Should I ask a customer's private business? Maybe she is planting a pea farm for a hobby. Or maybe she is starting a pea soup plant."

"Or a pea shooter plant?" laughed the Chief.

"Why not?" said Mr. Posey.

"Why not," agreed the Chief. "Well, Mr. Posey, I think we

have bothered you long enough." He untied Mr. Posey and his wife, and explained to Mr. Posey that even if he was running a one-hundred-percent-legal pea-packaging business, he would have to close his plant until the Pea Blockade was over.

"What difference does it make now?" said Mr. Posey. "I cannot clean up the mess you have made of my plant in less than a month."

"*Why not?*" shouted the Chief suddenly. "Why not? Why not?"

"Because it is a mess, that's why," yelled Mr. Posey.

"No, no, no, no," said the Chief. "Never mind the mess. I mean *why not* a pea shooter plant. For Wenda Gambling."

"What does Wenda Gambling want with a pea shooter plant?" asked Mr. Posey.

"Why not?" the Chief said again. "I mean, who knows. Do you have the bill for Miss Wanda Gambling's one ton of peas?"

"I have a carbon copy," said Mr. Posey.

"Let me see it," ordered the Chief.

The bill was made out to Miss Wanda Gambling at the Plaza Hotel. However, the Chief noticed that the one ton of peas had not been delivered to Wanda Gambling's apartment at the Plaza Hotel, but to Maxie Hammerman's shop.

The Chief pointed to Maxie's address. "Aha!" he said.

"Aha, what?" said Mr. Posey. He saw nothing odd about the order. He delivered peas to whatever address his customers requested.

"Maxie Hammerman, that's what," said the Chief.

"So?" said Mr. Posey. "Maybe they were a birthday present. Who is Maxie Hammerman?"

It happened that the Chief of the Pea-Tack Squad was one of the few people in New York City, outside of the pushcart peddlers and Maxie's personal friends, who knew who Maxie was.

"Maxie Hammerman," said the Chief thoughtfully, "is the Pushcart King."

CHAPTER XXII

The Raid on Maxie Hammerman's

Maxie Hammerman had no warning that the Pea-Tack Squad was going to raid his shop. The Squad, of course, found the shooters and all the ammunition that Maxie had stored in his cellar.

The Squad confiscated some five hundred pea shooters and half a ton of pea-tacks, and they arrested Maxie Hammerman. They could not arrest anyone else as they had no proof of anyone else being connected with the pea-tacks—except for

Wenda Gambling, and she was in Africa for a week's vacation.

At the word of Maxie's arrest, alarm spread among the pushcart peddlers. Fifty or sixty of them met after dark in a vacant lot under Manhattan Bridge to discuss the situation. They all expected to be arrested momentarily.

"What is there to discuss?" asked Papa Peretz. "It was a good war while it lasted. But now it is only a matter of time."

General Anna, however, refused to panic.

"What kind of talk am I hearing?" she demanded. "There is a little capture of some pea shooters, and suddenly everybody is surrendering. This is an *army*? I should be general of such an army?"

"It is just that things do not look so good," said Morris the Florist.

"*Good!*" said General Anna scornfully. "Did you think a war was going to be like a picnic in the country? A nice time for everybody?

"For weeks," General Anna pointed out, "we have been pushing back the trucks. Victory after victory. So now we have one little setback."

"*Little,*" said Mr. Jerusalem. "A five-hundred-pea-shooter raid is little?"

"Let them have the pea shooters," said General Anna. "At the moment we are not using them."

"But they have Maxie, too," Morris the Florist reminded General Anna.

"They also have Frank the Flower," said General Anna. "And Frank the Flower just sitting in jail is giving the trucks a great deal of trouble. A good man is a good man wherever he is sitting. And you can be sure that Maxie Hammerman is not sitting at Police Headquarters waiting to hear that we have surrendered."

"But what can we do?" asked Papa Peretz.

"In the first place, don't surrender," said General Anna. "In the second place, I will think of something."

General Anna paced up and down under the bridge for five or ten minutes, thinking to herself.

While General Anna was thinking, the confidence of the other peddlers began to return. Eddie Moroney and Carlos

133

gathered up some scrap lumber and built a bonfire. Harry the Hot Dog pushed his cart alongside the fire and broke open several packages of hots to be toasted over the fire. Carlos began to sing a song in Spanish that he said his son had made up. It was called "The Boy Who Killed a Thousand Trucks." There were thirty-six verses, all in Spanish, and everyone joined in on the chorus which went: *"Bravo, bravo, bravo!"*

"Bravo!" said General Anna, as she joined the others around the campfire.

"Have you thought of something?" asked Papa Peretz.

"I am going to communicate with Maxie Hammerman," said General Anna.

"How?" asked Mr. Jerusalem.

"I will send him a message in an apple," said General Anna. "Lend me your knife, Eddie Moroney."

General Anna selected a large apple from her cart and with Eddie's knife, she carefully cut the core out of the apple. Then she wrote a short message on a piece of paper and stuffed the paper in the apple. She cut a half-inch off the core and pushed the core back into place.

"Like a cork in a bottle," said Papa Peretz. "But how will we get the apple to Maxie?"

"I will give it to the Police Commissioner to deliver," said General Anna. "Is there a law an old lady shouldn't send an apple to a friend who has the misfortune to be in jail?"

"What is the message to Maxie about?" asked Eddie Moroney.

134

"Strategy," said General Anna firmly, and she took the apple down to police headquarters herself.

The Police Commissioner was used to people sending messages to prisoners. He told General Anna that he would deliver the apple, but before he delivered it, he inspected it very carefully.

When the Police Commissioner discovered that the core of the apple was loose, he pulled it out and read the message. However, he could not see that it would do any harm to deliver it.

"Remove the message before you eat the apple," the Police Commissioner advised when he gave the apple to Maxie.

Maxie Hammerman smiled when he found the message in the apple. The message read: "Good Luck! How is the blister on your thumb? Your friend Anna."

Maxie wrote back: "Thanks! The blister is okay. Give my regards to everybody. Your friend Maxie Hammerman."

The Police Commissioner read the reply and said that he would see that it got to Maxie's friend Anna.

"What does Maxie say?" asked Papa Peretz when General Anna received the reply.

"He sends regards," said General Anna.

"Is that all?" said Morris the Florist.

"The rest is strategy," said General Anna, which was encouraging to everyone.

Meantime, Frank the Flower had his own strategy. As soon as he heard from the guards in the jail about the raid on

Maxie's shop, he sent a message to the Police Commissioner. He informed the Commissioner that all the ammunition that the Pea-Tack Squad had confiscated belonged to him, and that his friend Maxie Hammerman had been letting him keep it in his cellar as a favor.

As soon as the Police Commissioner got Frank's message, he came down to Frank's jail cell to talk to Frank personally. Frank explained that he had been a good customer of Maxie's for many years.

"I have bought three pushcarts from Maxie Hammerman," said Frank the Flower, "and he makes all my repairs."

The Police Commissioner was inclined to believe Frank the Flower. It seemed reasonable to the Police Commissioner that a man who had shot down 18,991 trucks might have five hundred pea shooters hidden away somewhere. In addition, the Police Commissioner was not anxious to find a widespread conspiracy as that would make him look like a big dope all over again, and also would be a lot of trouble.

Unfortunately, the Pea-Tack Squad had found in Maxie's shop not only the ammunition Frank the Flower said belonged to him, but Maxie's big map with the red and gold pea-pins in it. The Police Commissioner had to admit that the map and certain notes that Maxie had made in the margins of the map did look suspicious.

The notes (Maxie's list of ace shots) read, "Harry the Hot Dog—230; Eddie Moroney—175; Morris the Florist—175; General Anna—160 (By Hand)."

The Police Commissioner could not make any sense out of the notes, but he guessed that they were a code that might explain the map. After studying the map for some time, he asked that Maxie Hammerman be brought to his office for questioning.

CHAPTER XXIII

The Questioning of Maxie Hammerman

The Police Commissioner questioned Maxie Hammerman in some detail. Maxie was very cooperative and did not refuse to answer any questions. The conversation, as recorded in the files of the New York City Police Department, went as follows:

Police Commissioner: Frank the Flower says that he is a friend of yours.

Maxie Hammerman: Why not? I got friends all over. As Pushcart King, I know everybody in the pushcart line.

P.C.: Why do they call you the Pushcart King?

M.H.: It is an honorary title. My father was Pushcart King, and I took over his business. My grandfather was also Pushcart King.

P.C.: Frank the Flower says that you have been storing a few items for him in your cellar.

M.H.: Why not? I like to do a favor for a friend if I can.

P.C.: Would you say that Frank the Flower is a crackpot?

M.H.: Why should I call a friend names? He has enough troubles.

P.C.: I have here what appears to be a map of the city of New York.

139

M.H.: Is it against the law to have a map of the city of New York?

P.C.: No. But I would like to know why you have such a map in your shop.

M.H.: Business reasons. It is a kind of business chart. As Pushcart King, I have to keep track of how business in the pushcart line is going.

P.C.: What are all those pea-tacks doing in the map?

M.H.: They are not pea-tacks. I have never seen a pea-tack in my life. Those are pea-pins in my map.

P.C.: Never mind what you call them. They are exactly like pea-tacks we have been finding in the truck tires and exactly like the pea-tacks you have been storing in your cellar for Frank the Flower.

M.H.: No, they are not. If you will examine them carefully, you will see that they are red, or once in a great while gold. Those you have found in the truck tires were white. At least, that is what I read in the newspapers.

P.C.: Red, gold, or white, what are they doing in that map?

M.H.: You have heard of "red-letter" days? Well, in my business I like to speak of "red-pin" days. It is the same idea. When a pushcart does a good business, I put a red pea-pin in the map where the business was good. If business is terrific, I put in a gold pea-pin. In this way, I know where in the city there has been the most activity.

P.C.: It is curious that the most activity on your map is in the same locations where the trucks have had the most flat tires.

M.H.: It stands to reason. When trucks break down, the traffic stops, so people cannot get to the stores uptown or downtown. When that happens, they buy from the pushcart closest at hand. Wherever there are flat tires, a pushcart does a good business.

P.C.: What does it mean at the bottom of the map where you have written in the margin: "Harry the Hot Dog—230"?

M.H.: I am often writing notes to myself. That could be a note to remind me that I have promised Harry the Hot Dog that his cart, which he has perhaps left for repairs, will maybe be finished at 230—that is to say, at 2:30 P.M.

P.C.: And "Eddie Moroney—175"? Maybe 1:75 P.M. is when Eddie Moroney's cart will be fixed?

M.H.: Certainly not. There is no such time as 1:75 P.M., as you should know. So "175" is more likely to be a note to remind me that I have told Eddie Moroney that for $1.75, I will put two new wheel spokes in his cart.

P.C.: And "General Anna—160 (By Hand)"—what does that mean?

M.H.: "By hand" is a peculiarity of General Anna. The note could be to remind me that I must fix Anna's cart by hand. Anna does not want any electric tools used on her cart. The cart was handmade in the first place by my father forty-two years ago, and Anna insists "only hand tools," such as the cart was built with in the first place. I can use a hammer, a saw, a screwdriver—as long as it is a hand tool. This is okay by me. I like working with my hands.

The Police Commissioner reported to Mayor Cudd that he had thoroughly questioned Maxie Hammerman and that he could find no reason to keep him under arrest.

THE PORTLETTE PAPERS

CHAPTER XXIV

The Portlette Papers: The LEMA Master Plan
& The Plot to Capture Maxie Hammerman
(From the Shorthand Notes of Miriam Portlette)

The truck drivers, when they heard that Maxie Hammerman had been released, were furious. At a meeting of The Three on May 17th, Big Moe, The Tiger and Louie Livergreen decided to take matters into their own hands. This involved a plot to kidnap Maxie Hammerman.

This plot is known because a cleaning woman, a young lady named Miriam Portlette, was cleaning an office next to the LEMA office where The Three met to plot against Maxie.

Miriam would have paid no attention to the discussion she heard through the open transom of Louie Livergreen's headquarters if it had not been that she was studying shorthand at an adult-education class on her nights off.

Miriam Portlette was studying shorthand in hopes of getting a better office job than the one she had. It was Miriam's ambition to have an office job with daytime hours so that she would not miss the evening television shows.

On the night that The Three met in Louie Livergreen's office, Miriam Portlette's shorthand assignment for the week was to take shorthand notes of a meeting. This assignment was a problem for Miriam. As she worked nights, she did not get to attend many meetings.

So when Miriam realized that some men were holding a meeting in the office next to the one that she was cleaning, she sat down on her mop bucket in the hall outside Louie Livergreen's office, and took down the whole meeting in shorthand notes on the backs of some order blanks that she had found in a wastebasket. The original copy of Miriam's notes (now known as "The Portlette Papers") is in the Rare Documents collection of the New York Public Library. A translation of the notes, by Miriam's shorthand teacher, reads as follows:

Shorthand notes of a meeting
by Miriam Portlette
Adult-Education Class 2-G
Seward Park High School

Dear Mr. Czerwinski*: Four men† are meeting together. Their names are Mr. Bigmo, Mr. Walter, Mr. Tiger, and Mr. Louie. I could not take shorthand notes of the very beginning of this meeting, as I had to look for some paper to make notes on. But the men were talking at first about ladies' hats and a movie star, and I do not think this was an important part of the meeting.

I think that the important part began when Mr. Louie said, "Let's get down to business." And, by then I had found some paper and a pencil.

---

* Miriam Portlette's shorthand teacher.
† It is clear from Miss Portlette's mention a few words later of a Mr. Walter and a Mr. Tiger that there were only three men (The Three) at the meeting. The fact that Big Moe called Walter Sweet "Tiger," while Louie Livergreen called him "Walter" gave Miriam the impression that there were four men in the office.

Mr. Louie: Let's get down to business. You called the meeting, Bigmo. What is the meeting about?

Mr. Bigmo: It is about Maxie Hammerman. I don't care what the Police Commissioner says. There is obviously a pushcart experiment.*

Mr. Walter: It is logical. The pushcarts have the best reason to be fighting the trucks of anyone in the city. The Police Commissioner does not know that. But we do.

Mr. Bigmo: So we have got to expose the experiment.†

Mr. Louie: Why expose? Expose, and it may be exposed that the trucks started it all by hitting the pushcarts.

Mr. Bigmo: So what do you suggest, Louie?

Mr. Louie: Do we have a Master Plan—or do we not? I do not want to waste any more time on the pushcarts.

Mr. Bigmo: Certainly, we have a Master Plan. We are all in favor of the LEMA Master Plan. But to get rid of the pushcarts is the first part of the Master Plan. Until we get rid of the pushcarts, we cannot get the trucks on the streets to carry out the second part of the Master Plan.

Mr. Louie: The pushcarts are easy. Maxie Hammerman, it is

---

* "Pushcart experiment" is probably a mistake in the notes. Undoubtedly, Big Moe said "pushcart conspiracy." One must remember that Miriam Portlette had never taken shorthand notes before, and also that she was seated in the hall outside Louie Livergreen's office.
† See note above.

146

clear, is the brains behind the pushcart experiment.* Get rid of Maxie Hammerman, and the rest of the peddlers will give up. I know pushcart peddlers. No fight. Would a man be in a small business like the pushcart business if he had any fighting spirit?

Mr. Tiger: Some people like a small business. They say you know the customers.

Mr. Louie: Customers! Who wants to know the customers? It is because they do not have the guts for a big business. And I guarantee—the pushcart peddlers would not be fighting without a very strong leader.

Mr. Bigmo: So we must get rid of Maxie Hammerman. As Louie says. But how?

Mr. Louie: We will kidnap him. Then we have a choice.

Mr. Bigmo: A choice?

Mr. Louie: A choice of how to get rid of him. We can torture him until he feels like giving the Police Commissioner a full confession that is guaranteed to get every pushcart peddler in the city locked up. Or, if he does not want to confess, he could just disappear, and we will knock off the rest of the pushcarts one by one.

Mr. Tiger: Do we have to kill off *all* the pushcarts? It is, after all, the cars and the taxis and the buses that are in our way. As you said, Louie, why waste time on the pushcarts?

Mr. Louie: We have to make an example of the pushcarts.

Mr. Tiger: An example?

---

* See note above.

Mr. Louie: Example, for example, for the cars and taxis. Example, for example, of what happens if a vehicle does not get out of the way of a truck. When we start on the cars, it is going to be tougher. The trucks are bigger, but there are four million cars in the city. And it will be very useful when we start on the cars, if all over the city people are whispering, "Remember what happened to the pushcarts?"

Mr. Bigmo: You understand, Tiger?

Mr. Louie: If we are going after four million cars, it is necessary that the cars should be scared when we start to hit them. They are a little bit afraid now. But not so afraid that they would give up without fighting.

Mr. Walter: To tell the truth, I am not so crazy about going after the cars.

Mr. Bigmo: But that is the idea of the Master Plan.

Mr. Louie: You have got to think ahead, Walter. There is not enough room for everybody in the streets. Why should people drive around the city for pleasure when they could take a bus? Get rid of the cars, and I can put two hundred Leaping Lemas on the streets. Get rid of the cars, and Big Moe can operate fifty more Mighty Mammoths and I don't know how many more Mama Mammoths and Baby Mammoths. And Tiger Trucking can put on the streets double the number of Ten-Ton Tigers you are now operating.

Mr. Tiger: Frankly, I got enough trucks now. It is just that traffic is so bad.

Mr. Bigmo: But that is the point, Tiger. Traffic is so bad that everybody will be wanting to get rid of the trucks if we do not get rid of them first.

Mr. Louie: You see, Walter, the Master Plan is in self-defense. We got no choice.

Mr. Walter: I suppose you are right, Louie. So the plan is we finish the pushcarts. Then the cars.

Mr. Bigmo: Then the taxis.

Mr. Louie: Then the small trucks.

Mr. Tiger: Trucks! But we are fighting to make the streets safe for the trucks.

Mr. Louie: For *big* trucks. Small trucks are as much nuisance as cars and taxis. They are not efficient. One Leaping Lema can take the place of five small trucks. A small truck is as bad as a pushcart.

Mr. Bigmo: Louie is right, Walter. Don't cry over small trucks.

Mr. Walter: But we have not told the truck drivers that small trucks are a part of the Master Plan. Half the trucks in the city are small trucks. A lot of truckers will not go along with the fight if it is going to be their funeral in the end.

Mr. Bigmo: So who's telling them? Listen, Walter the Tiger, the three of us have been friends for a long time. But if you do not stop talking like a small businessman, I am going to say that two heads are better than three.

Mr. Louie: We all agreed to the Master Plan a long time ago. Before the secret meeting in Moe Mammoth's garage.

Mr. Tiger: But when you told us the plan, Louie, you did not mention the small trucks.

Mr. Louie: It occurred to me later. Anyway we do not get to the small trucks until we take care of the cars and the taxis. And we cannot take care of them until we take care of Maxie Hammerman.

Mr. Walter: Who is going to kidnap Maxie?

Mr. Bigmo: We could each send half-a-dozen drivers.

Mr. Louie: No. The fewer people who know what has happened to Maxie Hammerman, the better. We will go ourselves.

Mr. Tiger: Just the three of us?

Mr. Bigmo: Three is not enough to take one man who is not expecting to be kidnapped?

Mr. Walter: When will we do it?

Mr. Louie: I am free next Friday night.

Mr. Bigmo: But that is the night we play cards with the Mayor.

Mr. Louie: Tell the Mayor we will have a late game.

Mr. Bigmo: All right. Now how shall we handle Maxie?

Mr. Louie: You want a Leaping Lema for the job?

Mr. Bigmo: No, Louie. We do not need a truck for a little trip like this. We will take my bulletproof Italian car.

The notes are signed:

> *Yours truly,*
> *Miriam Portlette*

P.S. (an explanation to her teacher): I did not stay to the end of the meeting as I had three more offices to mop, but I think it was almost over. *M. Portlette*

As far as Miriam Portlette was concerned, the meeting in Louie Livergreen's office was just a meeting. She did not know anything about the trucking business or the pushcart business. Nor had she heard that there was a war going on, because she did not read the newspapers and always missed the evening news on television, as she worked late.

Miriam simply copied down what The Three said at the meeting and turned in her notes to the teacher of her adult-education class. She had no idea that she had been present at a historic occasion.

The teacher of Miriam's adult-education class, however, did read the newspapers. And he listened to every news program on television.

In addition, Miriam's teacher lived next door to Eddie Moroney and went bowling with Eddie every Tuesday night. As a result, he was well informed about all the trouble that the pushcarts had been having with the trucks.

So when Miriam handed in her shorthand notes to be corrected, her teacher realized at once that they were important. He apparently copied them off—or at least those parts he could read—and he gave this copy of the notes to Eddie Moroney. Eddie, in turn, passed on the notes to Maxie Hammerman, and the notes undoubtedly saved Maxie's life.

CHAPTER XXV

*The Three-Against-One Gamble & The Capture of the
Bulletproof Italian Car*

Maxie Hammerman's handling of the plot to kidnap him
was one of the more brilliant strategies of the Pushcart War.
Eddie Moroney could not see the sense of it at first.

When Eddie gave Maxie Miriam Portlette's shorthand
notes of the meeting of The Three, Eddie suggested that
Maxie give them to a newspaper reporter.

"If the LEMA Master Plan is published in a newspaper,"
Eddie said, "then everyone will see what is happening."

Maxie laughed. "Who would believe it, Eddie? That three
men have a plan to kill all the cars and taxis in New York
City? Nobody wants to believe such a terrible thing. The
Three would deny it, and the only thing that would happen
is that I would disappear that much sooner."

"Maybe you are right," Eddie said. "But in any case you
are not going to disappear next Friday night. Since we know
about that part of the Master Plan, you can be a long way from
the shop next Friday night."

"Certainly not," said Maxie.

"You do not believe the Master Plan yourself?" Eddie
asked.

"Believe me, I believe it," said Maxie. "But this is what I
believe also. I believe that the only way to win a war is to be
on hand for the battle wherever it is going to be."

"On hand?" said Eddie.

"On hand in my shop," said Maxie, "when Big Moe in his bulletproof Italian car comes looking for me."

"Oh," said Eddie. "Well, if that is the idea, a number of people will be on hand. When The Three come looking for you on Friday night, there will be Harry the Hot Dog and Morris the Florist and Carlos and one or two others in the backroom of your shop to greet them."

"No," said Maxie. "I will greet them by myself."

"But that will be a three-against-one fight," said Eddie.

"I am gambling," said Maxie, "that one head is sometimes better than three."

"Gambling is fine," said Eddie Moroney. "But we cannot afford to lose your head. Therefore I am coming on Friday night to watch you gamble. In case something should happen. Some little emergency."

"All right," said Maxie. "That would be a comfort to me. Especially as you have worked with a circus and can, no doubt, handle lions and tigers in an emergency."

"I only lettered the posters for the circus," said Eddie Moroney.

"Never mind," said Maxie. "That takes more brains."

"All the same," said Eddie Moroney, "I would just as soon we had one or two men besides myself on Friday night."

"I appreciate the advice," said Maxie. "However, for the time being, I do not want you to tell the other pushcart peddlers about the shorthand notes of Miriam Portlette. My only question is, can you play poker?"

Eddie said that he could.

"Good," said Maxie. "Come to my shop at seven o'clock on Friday night and bring a new deck of playing cards." That was all Maxie would tell Eddie Moroney about his plans.

Maxie then called the Police Commissioner. As he had parted from the Police Commissioner on friendly terms, Maxie suggested that the Commissioner drop around to his shop on Friday night for a friendly game of poker.

"I only play for money," said the Police Commissioner.

"I like to gamble myself," said Maxie Hammerman.

The Police Commissioner agreed to come then, especially as there were a few more questions he wanted to ask Maxie about Frank the Flower.

"To tell the truth, I have not had too much experience with crackpots," said the Police Commissioner, "but it does not seem to me that Frank is a hopeless case."

"Probably not," said Maxie. "And I will answer any questions I can."

So on Friday night, the evening The Three had set to kidnap Maxie Hammerman, Maxie was sitting down in the back room of his shop with his friend Eddie Moroney and the Police Commissioner for a friendly game of poker. The Police Commissioner had just drawn four aces when the door to the back room opened and in walked Big Moe and The Tiger and Louie Livergreen, all with their hands in their right overcoat pockets, from which Eddie Moroney guessed that they all carried guns.

The Three were so surprised to see the Police Commissioner

that they could not decide whether to take their hands out of their pockets or not. The Police Commissioner, who never bothered with polite conversation with anyone who had a hand in his right overcoat pocket, jumped to his feet and pulled his own gun.

However, before the Police Commissioner could shoot, Maxie stepped in front of him and said, "Hello, Moe. Hello, Louie. Hello, Walter the Tiger. I have been expecting you."

As The Three had never set eyes on Maxie Hammerman in person before, and as he—to their knowledge—had never set eyes on them, Maxie's calling them by their first names scared even Louie Livergreen. And when Maxie held out his hand, Louie could not do anything but take his hand out of his pocket and shake Maxie's hand.

"Meet my friend the Police Commissioner," Maxie said. "Commissioner, these are my good friends who have just dropped in to play a little poker with us."

"Moe Mammoth is a friend of yours?" said the Police Commissioner. The Commissioner was still annoyed about Big Moe's calling him a big dope to the newspapers.

"A poker-playing friend," said Maxie. "We have differences of opinion, but we get together for a friendly game of poker.

"As you perhaps know," Maxie explained to the Police Commissioner, "Big Moe and The Tiger and Mr. Livergreen usually play a friendly game of cards with Mayor Emmett P. Cudd on Friday night. So we should be honored that they have come to play at my shop instead."

And before The Three knew what was happening, **Eddie Moroney** was politely helping them off with their overcoats which he hung up on the wall nearest Maxie Hammerman. The Police Commissioner started to put his gun back in his holster but, on second thought, laid it on the table beside him.

"There is just one little matter of business before we start our game," Maxie said as he shuffled the cards.

The Three exchanged nervous looks.

"What business is that?" Big Moe asked.

"Did you bring the bulletproof Italian car?" asked Maxie Hammerman.

At the mention of a bulletproof Italian car, the Police Commissioner put his hand on his gun.

"It is nothing to worry about," Maxie assured the Police Commissioner. "It is just that Big Moe has agreed to sell me his bulletproof Italian car, as he has no further need of it. Whereas, a man in my position cannot be too careful.

"You have the car outside?" Maxie asked.

"It's in front of the shop," Big Moe said warily.

"Good," said Maxie Hammerman. "Maybe I should have my friend the Police Commissioner fire one or two shots into the side to test whether it is really bulletproof. However, I trust you."

Maxie took a check from his pocket and laid it on the table. "I have here a check for $14.50 made out to Mr. Moe Mammoth for one bulletproof Italian car. Is that correct?"

"Big Moe is selling you a bulletproof car for $14.50?" said the Police Commissioner suspiciously.

"It's secondhand," said Maxie. "And we are friends." He passed the check across the table to Big Moe.

Big Moe looked at Louie Livergreen to see what he should do, but Louie was watching the Police Commissioner tapping the handle of his gun and offered no advice.

"Take it," whispered The Tiger.

So Big Moe picked up the check.

"If you will just give me a receipt," said Maxie Hammerman, "saying 'paid in full for one bulletproof Italian car, secondhand,' we can get on with the card game."

Eddie Moroney gave Big Moe a pen, and Big Moe wrote out the receipt.

158

"I hope everybody has had a good week's business," said Maxie, as he dealt the cards, "and can afford to make a few sporting bets, as I promised my friend the Police Commissioner a good game."

"I hope so, too," said the Police Commissioner, scowling at Big Moe. "I have never liked a man who talks like a big shot to the newspapers and then makes very small bets when he is at the poker table."

With the Police Commissioner's gun on the table and their overcoats on the wall beside Maxie Hammerman, The Three did not want to annoy the Police Commissioner by making any small bets. Fortunately, it was Friday night and The Three had in their pockets whatever amount of their profits they took home with them at the end of every week.

"Of course, it has been a bad week," said Big Moe, in case the Police Commissioner did not think the bets were big enough.

The Police Commissioner won the first three hands. His winnings were $237, most of which he won from The Three, as Eddie and Maxie did not bet much on the first three hands.

"For a big dope, you are a pretty good poker player," Maxie said to the Police Commissioner.

The Police Commissioner did not mind Maxie Hammerman calling him a big dope.

Eddie Moroney won the next hand and got $42 from Louie Livergreen. Louie had three queens and Eddie Moroney only had two jacks, but Eddie was so determined not to

159

give in to Louie that Louie got nervous and threw in his hand.

Then Maxie Hammerman started winning. He won every one of the next ten hands, winning each time larger amounts, as The Three made bigger and bigger bets, hoping to stop Maxie. On the last hand alone, Maxie's winnings were $13,500, and altogether Maxie won over $60,000.

Big Moe lost the most money to Maxie. He even bet the $14.50 check Maxie had written him and lost that. The game had to stop then as none of The Three had any more money in their pockets.

"Now that is what I call a conspiracy," laughed the Police Commissioner, as he helped Maxie sort out the $60,000 into piles of ten, fifty, and hundred dollar bills. Big Moe was look-ing so foolish that the Police Commissioner did not begrudge Maxie a cent of his winnings.

"And," he said to Big Moe, "if you wish me to investigate this conspiracy, I will be glad to do so, as it would be worth my time to know how Maxie Hammerman won so much money on ten hands of poker."

The Police Commissioner then offered to take The Three home in a squad car as they did not have any money for bus fare. "If anyone sees you riding in the squad car," he said, "I will explain that you are not common criminals."

CHAPTER XXVI

Maxie Hammerman's War Chest: A Philosophy of War

Maxie Hammerman has sometimes been portrayed as a happy-go-lucky fighter whose victory over The Three on the night they came to kidnap him was a matter of pure luck. Maxie himself has always been modest about his part in the Pushcart War. From his own descriptions of the $60,000 card game, one might easily conclude that Maxie was simply a crazy gambler who was lucky enough to hold the right cards.

However, Eddie Moroney, who was there, guarantees that Maxie knew what he was doing at every step of the game. Eddie remembers a conversation with Maxie just after The Three had left with the Police Commissioner.

Eddie and Maxie were having a bottle of cream soda together, and Eddie said to Maxie, "I, also, would like to know, Maxie, how you won so much money on ten hands of poker, as I know you do not cheat at cards."

"It is simple," Maxie said. "I won all the money because Louie Livergreen—of whom The Tiger and Big Moe are a little afraid—because he is the one who makes all the plans—was afraid of me.

"Louie was afraid of me," Maxie explained, "because he knows I could have had the Police Commissioner shoot him on the spot for breaking into my shop. But I did not. Instead, I pretended that Louie and Big Moe and The Tiger were my friends, by which Louie Livergreen knew that *I* was not afraid of him. And this scared Louie Livergreen. Because if I am not afraid of him, it means that either I am smarter than he is, or that I have made a plan which is even better, from my point of view, than to have the Police Commissioner shoot him.

"So," Maxie smiled, "Louie Livergreen's mind was not on the cards he was playing, and Big Moe and The Tiger could see that Louie Livergreen was nervous, which made them nervous, and they did not play their cards carefully.

"Also," said Maxie, "I played my cards very carefully."

"It was a good game," said Eddie. "But I still do not understand why you did not let the Police Commissioner shoot them. It would have been such a surprise to them."

"Yes," said Maxie, "but it would have been against my philosophy of war."

"In what way?" Eddie asked.

"In this way," said Maxie. "Louis Livergreen, you may recall, thought that if he kidnapped me, the pushcart peddlers would not fight."

"We would fight harder," said Eddie Moroney indignantly.

"Certainly," said Maxie Hammerman.

"In the same way," Maxie pointed out, "if we got rid of Big Moe and Louie and The Tiger, there would still be maybe a million truck drivers who hate the pushcarts. Also, there are three other men behind The Three who would be only too happy to see Big Moe and Louie and The Tiger disappear so that they could be the top three. I can name you twelve men who would fight with each other to be the top three.

"It is my idea." Maxie went on, "that if you are going to have enemies, it is better to have enemies you already know. It is easier to guess what they are going to do.

"Also," said Maxie, "it is better to have enemies who have learned to be a little afraid of you."

Maxie scooped up the $60,000 he had won and stuffed it into an old tool chest. Then he dipped his finger in a can of axle oil and lettered on the side of the box "WAR CHEST."

"What is that for?" asked Eddie Moroney.

"My philosophy of war," Maxie continued, "is that what you need to win a war is money. Everybody is willing to fight for a good cause. Fine. But there comes a time when you run out of money for peas—for pins—for whatever you are using

for ammunition at the moment. You cannot afford the repairs to your pushcart. Or for the doctor bills when you get hurt in the fighting. Or, to feed the children because you cannot work a regular schedule. There comes a time.

"When that time comes," Maxie said, "we have this war chest. Anyone who cannot afford to pay me for repairs to his pushcart may take from this chest. No questions asked. As long as he is fighting, the money is there."

"You mean we are going to pay you to fix our carts with your own money which you won at poker?" said Eddie.

"Who knows it is my money?" asked Maxie. "Who needs to know? It is from contributions to our war effort."

"But who would contribute to us?" Eddie asked.

"Why not?" said Maxie. "I am the Pushcart King. Kings can get contributions.

"And a king, Eddie Moroney," Maxie said, looking very pleased with himself, "a king takes care of his people in time of war. You should know that."

Eddie Moroney pulled from his pocket the $42 he had won from Louie Livergreen and gave it to Maxie Hammerman. "It is a contribution," Eddie said.

"To the Pushcart King for the Pushcart War," he added.

CHAPTER XXVII

The Truck Drivers' Manifesto

After the failure of the plot to capture Maxie Hammerman, The Three were not anxious to tangle directly with Maxie again. They decided to attack in a different way.

They called a meeting of all the truck drivers in the city. At this meeting the drivers drew up a manifesto which they sent to Mayor Cudd. The manifesto claimed that Maxie Hammerman's map and the fact the ammunition had been found in his basement was clear evidence of a pushcart conspiracy.

The manifesto made four demands:

1. That every pushcart peddler in the city be arrested;
2. That pushcarts be permanently banned from the streets as they were endangering the whole city;
3. That Maxie Hammerman be fined $60,000 and sentenced to 60 years in jail for organizing the Pushcart Conspiracy, and
4. That the Police Commissioner be fired, as there was reason to believe he was in on the whole conspiracy.

The truck drivers warned that if the Mayor did not act at once along the lines suggested, they would have no choice but to declare war on the pushcarts. Mayor Cudd called the Police Commissioner and read him the manifesto.

"Well, what do you want me to do?" asked the Commissioner. "If you fire me, I cannot arrest the peddlers."

The Mayor had not thought of that. "I think the truck

drivers would settle for arresting the pushcart peddlers," he said. "At least, that is Point One of the manifesto."

"Well, I cannot arrest the pushcart peddlers in any case," said the Police Commissioner. "There are, according to Maxie Hammerman, over five hundred pushcart peddlers in this city, and we do not have that many empty cells in the jail.

"Moreover," said the Police Commissioner, "even if there *were* a pushcart conspiracy, it would be impossible to prove which trucks have been shot down by pushcart peddlers as a part of the conspiracy and which have been shot down by children purely in a spirit of fun.

"Do you want me to arrest all the children, too?" asked the Police Commissioner. "Including those whose fathers are truck drivers?"

"No, no," said the Mayor. "Just the pushcart peddlers."

"Well, I am not going to arrest *anybody* without proof," said the Police Commissioner, "including Maxie Hammerman, who is a gentleman, a good sport, and a good businessman. Once I start arresting people without proof, what is to stop me from arresting you?"

"Me?" said the Mayor nervously.

"But what can I do?" pleaded the Mayor. "Fifty thousand truck drivers have signed this manifesto. That is fifty thousand votes, you know."

"I suggest that you declare a truce until the question of a conspiracy can be fully investigated," said the Police Commissioner. "If any pushcart peddler violates the truce, I will arrest him—but not before."

CHAPTER XXVIII

The Truce

The period of the truce was a difficult time for the push-cart peddlers. They had won the first battle, but they had not won the war. The peddlers realized that within a week all the truck tires would have been repaired and that the trucks would be on the streets again in full force and more determined than ever to make trouble for the pushcarts.

This was exactly what happened. Within a week Maxie Hammerman's shop was filled with pushcarts needing repairs of all sorts. If it had not been for Maxie's war chest, many of the peddlers would have lost heart entirely.

167

One day General Anna had a wheel ripped off her cart by a truck crowding her into a curb. Maxie Hammerman said that Anna would need a new cart as there was damage to the axle that could not be repaired.

The pushcart peddlers held a meeting to discuss the truce. Morris the Florist pounded on a table. "When they hit a lady," he said, "it is too much! What kind of truce is that?"

"General Anna has had that cart for forty-two years," said Maxie Hammerman. "My father built it when I was just learning to use a hammer."

"Forty-two years, and I never had a day's trouble with it," said General Anna. "Maxie's father once said to me, 'When I build a cart, it could last a lifetime.' So maybe I should die now."

"Please don't, General Anna," said Papa Peretz.

"Naturally I won't," said General Anna. "I wouldn't give a truck the satisfaction. I was used to that cart. But never mind. Maxie Hammerman can build me another. What I want to know is: Why don't we fight back as before? Just selling apples and pears while a truck is cutting off my wheel, I don't like so much."

"I am perfectly willing to fight back," said Harry the Hot Dog.

" 'Willing' is not the question," said Maxie Hammerman. "If we break the truce, we are in serious trouble. The Police Commissioner has promised the Mayor that he will arrest anyone who breaks the truce."

"A truck is smashing my axle and it is a *truce?*" said General Anna.

"You are right," said Maxie Hammerman. "But how can you prove that it was not an accident? And any accidental damage we do the trucks now would be very risky. The truck drivers are looking for just one good excuse to make the Mayor put us off the streets entirely."

"Maxie is right," said Mr. Jerusalem. "We must not damage the trucks at this time. But I have an idea. We can make a peaceful protest."

"*Peaceful!*" said General Anna scornfully. "Peaceful like a broken axle?"

Mr. Jerusalem shook his head. "Like a Peace March," he

said. "What I mean is this: the trucks want to run us down one at a time when nobody is looking. They hit General Anna, and everybody says it is an accident."

"That we already know," said Harry the Hot Dog.

"I am coming to something else," said Mr. Jerusalem. "Suppose a truck has to run down one hundred and seventy pushcarts at a time. Could that be an accident?"

"So we should all get killed?" said General Anna. "Is that what you are coming to?"

"For once, listen," said Mr. Jerusalem. "My idea is as follows: we choose three streets, three streets where there is always a lot of truck traffic. We divide into *three* teams—one hundred and seventy pushcarts to a team. Then we go marching down these three streets, one team down each street. We are lined up across the street, six or seven pushcarts in a row—like a parade."

"Or like an army," said General Anna. "An army of three divisions. Call it an army, and I like the idea. So continue," she added.

Mr. Jerusalem continued. "We have filled the streets where we are marching. No truck has room to pass us. A truck driver comes driving toward us. He says, 'Out of my way, Pushcarts.' But we keep marching forward. Very peaceful. Doing business as usual." Mr. Jerusalem paused to let everyone get the picture.

Papa Peretz looked doubtful. "And while we are doing business as usual, the truck keeps coming forward?"

"So he keeps coming," said Mr. Jerusalem. "Are we worried? No. To push us out of the way, that truck would have to run down six, twelve, eighteen, forty, maybe one hundred and seventy pushcarts to get through that street. Could that be an accident?" Mr. Jerusalem demanded.

"No," he replied triumphantly. "It could not! And so the truck drivers will have to bargain with us. They will have to guarantee no more hitting the pushcarts."

"*Bargain* with us," said Harry the Hot Dog. "They would rather run us down—six, twelve, eighteen, *forty* pushcarts. What do they care how many they hit?"

"Ah," said Mr. Jerusalem, "but if they *do* hit us, then everyone will *see* who is breaking the truce. Who could hit forty carts by accident? I say they will not dare."

"But if they do—?" said Harry the Hot Dog.

Mr. Jerusalem shrugged. "Then six, twelve, eighteen, forty pushcarts will be smashed," he said. "Maybe we will all be killed. It is a war, isn't it?"

"A *Peace* March you are calling this!" said Harry the Hot Dog.

"Are *we* hitting anyone?" asked Mr. Jerusalem. "Are we breaking any law?"

"Yes," said Morris the Florist. "If the trucks are coming toward us and we are marching *toward* the trucks, and it is a one-way street, which it certainly will be, we will be going the *wrong* way down a one-way street—and *that* is against the law."

Mr. Jerusalem laughed. "A minor traffic violation," he said. "Nothing serious, like breaking a truce."

"Nothing serious," General Anna agreed. "In fact, it is a fine plan, and I am marching in the front line. You could hurry with the pushcart, Maxie?"

CHAPTER XXIX

The Peace March

Maxie Hammerman was able to finish General Anna's new pushcart in time for the Peace March by using, with General Anna's permission, his electric drill and power saw. It was true what Maxie Hammerman had told the Police Commissioner about General Anna's preferring the work on her cart to be done by hand.

"But we are at war," said General Anna. "It is more important that I should have the cart in time for the Peace March."

Maxie Hammerman said afterward that the greatest compliment anyone ever paid him was General Anna's remark when she saw her cart: "Even with electric tools, Maxie Hammerman can make a cart every bit as good as his father made by hand." Maxie was so proud of this compliment that he personally bought General Anna a cartful of the best-quality apples and pears, so that she would make the best appearance possible on the day of the Peace March.

As Mr. Jerusalem had suggested, the Peace Army was divided into three groups of about one hundred and seventy pushcarts each. Mr. Jerusalem was to lead the First Division down West Street. Harry the Hot Dog commanded the Second Division which was going to march down Broome Street. General Anna herself took charge of the Third Division which was to march down Greene Street.

General Anna gave orders that all divisions were to report to their stations at 7:30 on the morning of the Peace March so that they could get lined up before there was any amount of traffic in the streets. This meant that some of the peddlers had to set out before dawn to reach the street where their division was to march.

The Peace March was well organized. The peddlers had all dressed in their best clothes and many of the carts had been freshly painted for the occasion. A few peddlers in each division carried posters and some of the carts displayed banners.

The banners and posters had been lettered by Eddie Moroney. The lettering looked very professional because of Eddie's long experience in lettering circus carts and posters as a young man before he went into the pushcart line.

The banners all read: "PEACE MARCH," some in plain and some in circus-type lettering. The posters, however, said different things: "Be Fair to the Pushcarts" or "Don't Push the Pushcarts Around," or simply "Pushcarts for Peace."

Some of the posters were gaily decorated with birds and flowers and other designs Eddie Moroney felt were in keeping with a peace march. General Anna thought a lion or two would be very nice, as Eddie Moroney was known to be very good at drawing lions as well as at lettering. But Eddie said lions definitely were not in keeping with a peace march.

The Peace March was almost entirely peaceful. With the First and Second Divisions, everything went exactly as Mr. Jerusalem had predicted.

The truck drivers who found themselves confronted by the First and Second Divisions stopped their trucks. When the peddlers in the front lines refused to let the trucks through, and when the truck drivers saw that there were three or four solid blocks of pushcarts backing up the front lines, they realized that there was nothing they could do.

They agreed among themselves that they could not smash their way through a street full of pushcarts, even if they were angry enough to wish to. It was not that the trucks could not have broken a path through the carts. The difficulty was that while the drivers had been arguing with the peddlers about letting them pass, the banners and posters had attracted large numbers of people. If the drivers had challenged the Peace Army and anyone had been hurt, it would have been quite clear to the spectators that the truck drivers had rammed the carts intentionally.

It was annoying to the drivers to have to give in to the push-cart peddlers. But they had no choice. Traffic had piled up so rapidly behind them that they could not even turn around and drive off in the opposite direction.

So on both Broome and West Streets, the drivers were forced to agree, however bad-humoredly, to the condition named by Mr. Jerusalem and Harry the Hot Dog. This was simply a promise to ask The Three to meet with Maxie Hammerman and work out a peaceful settlement of the problems that had led to the Pushcart War.

One of the truck drivers warned Mr. Jerusalem that even if The Three did agree to talk with Maxie Hammerman that

that was no guarantee that the pushcarts would get what they wanted.

Mr. Jerusalem smiled. "Maybe not," he said. "But it is a beginning. To talk is better than to fight."

"Also," added Papa Peretz, "if the talk is not helpful, we can march again."

After the truck drivers had promised to ask The Three to meet with Maxie Hammerman, Papa Peretz gave each of them a bag of pretzels as a token of good will. At about the same time, over on Broome Street, Harry the Hot Dog was passing out free hot dogs.

Then Mr. Jerusalem and Harry the Hot Dog signalled their divisions that they were to turn their carts around and march peacefully down the block, clearing the street for the truck drivers. At the about-face signal from their leaders, all the peddlers swung their carts around.

As the pushcarts could not move very fast, the trucks had to creep along behind them for some blocks. Thus, it appeared to onlookers along the sidewalks as if the pushcarts of the First and Second Divisions were leading triumphal parades—which, in a way, they were. When people occasionally clapped their hands, Papa Peretz bowed to the right and left like the main actor in a play, which encouraged people to clap even harder and once or twice to break into cheers.

Down on Greene Street, however, the Third Division was running into trouble. The first truck to be challenged by the Third Division of the Peace Army was, unfortunately, driven by Albert P. Mack. Mack was driving the same Mighty Mammoth that had hit Morris the Florist's cart at the very beginning of the Pushcart War.

CHAPTER XXX

Mack's Attack

When Mack saw the army of pushcart peddlers in front of him, he thought at first he was having a bad dream. Mack had been having bad dreams about pushcarts ever since he had hit Morris the Florist.

Mack thought he must be dreaming now because he was on a one-way street. He knew *he* was going in the right direction, and he could see in his rear-view mirror at least six other trucks behind him. *Seven* trucks, Mack reasoned, could not be going the wrong way down a street they traveled every day.

Very much confused, Mack kept on going until he was

179

within ten feet of the pushcarts. He did stop then, tramping on his brake so suddenly that the truck following him whammed him a terrific blow from behind.

There was a shattering of glass that sounded like a thousand punch bowls cracking up—which is exactly what it was— Mack was loaded with punch bowls that morning. Mack himself was flung against his steering wheel so hard that for a minute he was certain he had broken a rib. He gasped and blinked and peered groggily down at the pushcarts.

They were certainly no dream. They stretched in a solid mass as far as he could see. Mack was furious. He socked his horn, warning the Peace Army to move aside and let him through.

No one moved. General Anna, her new cart heaped high with the best-quality apples Maxie Hammerman had bought her, was in the very center of the front line. She simply stood there eating an apple as if she had all the time in the world.

Mack realized that the peddlers had not the least intention of letting him through. "What's the big idea?" he bellowed from his cab.

"Read for yourself," said General Anna, negligently tossing the apple core at one of Mack's front tires. "It says on the signs."

Mack could see the signs all right, but he was not interested in reading them.

"Get off the street!" he shouted. But none of the peddlers paid him the least attention. Some of them were doing a good business with people who had gathered to watch the Peace March.

Several other truck drivers, who had pulled up behind Mack, had climbed out of their cabs and come up to see what the trouble was. General Anna explained to them that the peddlers would let them through if the drivers promised to let the peddlers use the streets in peace.

"Why should we promise you anything?" demanded one of the drivers.

"Because if you do not, we will not let you pass," said General Anna. "Suit yourself."

"You trying to start a fight, lady?" asked one of the drivers.

"When there is a truce?" said General Anna, looking very shocked. "Certainly not. I am just going to stay here peacefully with my pushcart. My friends will do the same."

The drivers did not know what to do. They went back to consult with Mack who had refused even to get out of his truck to argue with the peddlers.

"I'm going through," Mack said.

"You can't, Mack," said one of the other drivers. "There are too many of them."

"There'll be fewer in a minute," said Mack, starting his engine.

"Wait, Mack, wait!" begged his friend. "You're crazy!"

Mack hesitated. He looked down at the Peace Army. Unluckily, his eye fell on Morris the Florist who was standing in the front line next to General Anna.

Mack had had a grudge against Morris ever since he had smashed Morris' cart, for he felt that Morris had put him in a bad light with his wife. Mack's wife had told him that driving a big truck did not give him the right to bully everyone else on the street.

So when Mack saw Morris in the front line with a new pushcart, the idea of the same pushcart peddler blocking his way a *second* time threw him into a rage. Without taking his eye off Morris, Mack revved his engine and let go his brake.

"Look out," he yelled. "I'm coming through!"

Two truck drivers jumped onto Mack's running board and grabbed his arm. Mack flung them off.

"They're obstructing the street," he growled. "Can't you see? It's illegal."

"But there are at least two hundred of them," said one of his friends. "Can't you *see* that?"

"I can see," Mack said and his voice grew frighteningly calm. "The thing is—this truck weighs twenty thousand pounds when it is empty—and it is now fully loaded."

Mack stepped on the accelerator. The two drivers who had tried to reason with him backed away, and Mack drove straight into the Peace Army.

There was a terrible splintering and cracking as pushcarts buckled and shattered and flew into the air. Onlookers screamed as slats, wheels, apples, used clothing, and dancing dolls rained down on them.

Fortunately, a pushcart axle, wrenched free by the collision

184

of pushcarts and truck, was hurled, as if by design, straight through Mack's windshield. The axle missed Mack's head by less than an inch, but he lost control of the truck. The Mighty Mammoth swerved, plunged over the curb, sheared off a fire hydrant and crashed through a plate glass window into a cafeteria.

Miraculously, no one was killed. General Anna and Morris the Florist, who had been in the center of the line, directly in the path of the truck, had fallen to the ground so that the truck, although it shattered their carts, passed right over them.

Morris would have been killed if it had not been for General Anna. General Anna seized Morris by the hand and dragged him to the ground. Morris had been so stunned by the realization that he was about to be run down for the *second* time in three months by the *same* truck driver, that he had stood frozen with astonishment in the path of the truck. Only General Anna's quick thinking saved his life.

The peddlers directly behind Anna and Morris had a few seconds in which to run to the sides of the street, although they could not, of course, save their carts. About eighty carts were wrecked and a number of others were seriously damaged. There were a few broken arms and broken legs and any number of nasty cuts and bruises. But it could have been very much worse.

Forty thousand dollars' worth of damage was done to the cafeteria alone, and the proprietor estimated that several hundred people would have been killed if all his customers had not rushed out to the street minutes before the crash to hear Mack's argument with the Peace Army. Mack was immediately arrested for reckless driving, and there were plenty of witnesses eager to tell the police that Mack had run down the pushcarts on purpose.

Despite their losses, the pushcart peddlers were in good spirits. They felt certain that Mack's attack on the Third Division had demonstrated for once and for all who was to blame for the trouble in the streets. Eddie Moroney lifted General Anna onto his pushcart and personally pushed her all the way back to Maxie Hammerman's shop for a victory celebration. However, that celebration was never held.

CHAPTER XXXI
The Sneak Attack

By the time the battered but jubilant Third Division arrived at Maxie's shop, Mayor Cudd had begun the desperate sneak attack that was intended to wipe out the whole pushcart army at one blow.

The Third Division arrived at Maxie's to find their friends from the First and Second Divisions listening in shocked disbelief to a radio announcement by the Mayor. Mayor Cudd was announcing that he had suspended all pushcart licenses until further notice.

"An army is an army," Mayor Cudd was saying, "whether it calls itself a Peace Army or some other kind of army. And it is my view that the pushcart peddlers, in organizing an army, have violated the truce.

"They have provoked violence and bad feeling," said Mayor Cudd. "Not to mention the disruption of traffic on three streets of our city, and the destruction of public property."

"What are you talking about, you crazy Cudd?" shouted General Anna, seizing Maxie Hammerman's portable radio and shaking it in terrible anger.

"I am talking, of course, about the destruction of a fire hydrant on Greene Street," Mayor Cudd's voice continued.

"A hydrant was destroyed?" Maxie asked, as he had not

187

heard all the details of Mack's attack on the Peace Army.

"By a truck, of course," said Morris the Florist. "The usual smashing."

"The Fire Commissioner is extremely upset," the Mayor went on. "Water is flooding Greene Street, and he has had five men there for an hour trying to seal off the water main."

"*The Fire Commissioner* is upset," General Anna screamed at the radio. "*That* is the worst thing that has happened to-day?" and she would have thrown the radio on the floor if Maxie Hammerman had not taken it firmly out of her hands and led her gently to a chair.

"And I am disturbed, too," the Mayor proceeded. "Therefore, I am not only temporarily suspending all pushcart licenses, but I am also recommending to the City Council when it meets next week that these licenses be permanently revoked."

The peddlers stared blankly at the radio as the Mayor went on to express his sympathy to Mack's family and to all truck drivers who had been inconvenienced by the Peace March. The Mayor expressed regret at Mack's arrest and said that he would do everything he could to see that he was released promptly.

Meantime, the Mayor said, he trusted that the citizens of the city appreciated the courage of this great driver's standing up to his traffic rights when he was so pitifully outnumbered. "Think of it," said the Mayor, "—one truck driver against hundreds of pushcarts!"

As for the promises extracted from the truckers by the First and Second Divisions, the Mayor said Mr. Mammoth had already assured him that he and Mr. Livergreen and Mr. Sweet had no intention of meeting with Maxie Hammerman. These law-abiding men, the Mayor explained, could hardly be expected to honor a promise made as a result of a Peace March that was a clear violation of a sacred truce.

At this point Mr. Jerusalem rose and, without a word, picked up one of Maxie's hammers and smashed the radio to bits.

The rest of the peddlers were too stunned to even discuss the incredible turn of events. Maxie urged everyone to return home as quietly and quickly as possible, and to get his cart off the street, for the Mayor's action had put them all in danger of arrest at any moment.

As Mr. Jerusalem had no place to put his cart but on the street, Maxie insisted that he spend the night at the Hammerman shop. It was the first time in seventy years that Mr. Jerusalem had slept indoors, and it made him feel like an old man.

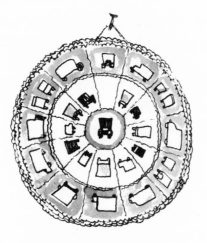

CHAPTER XXXII

Frank the Flower's Crocheted Target

The Three left Mayor Cudd's headquarters on the night of the Peace March confident that the Pushcart War was as good as won. The Mayor's broadcast, they felt sure, would break the back of any further resistance on the part of the pushcart peddlers.

In fact, The Three left Mayor Cudd's to map their plans for Operation Krushkar (the code name for the autumn automobile offensive that was scheduled as the second stage of the LEMA Master Plan). The Three could hardly have foreseen at this point the possible significance of a psychological victory that Frank the Flower was to score over Albert P. Mack during the time the latter was held prisoner. But the resulting damage to Mack's morale—and to their own, when they heard it—may have had a critical effect on the events of the next few weeks.

On being arrested, Mack had been locked in a cell directly across from Frank the Flower's. This, in itself, had enraged Mack. While he was glad to see that Frank the Flower was still in jail, it angered him that Frank should have the similar pleasure of seeing him in jail.

From the moment he was locked up, Mack had been throwing temper tantrums, kicking at the walls of the cell, bellowing into the corridor, insulting the guards, and in general making a nuisance of himself. When the Police Commissioner was summoned to see what the guards were complaining about, Mack kicked him in the shins.

The Police Commissioner decided that Mack was definitely a criminal type. And when Mayor Cudd, as he had promised, personally requested that Mack be released, the Police Commissioner refused.

Mayor Cudd maintained that as he had declared the Peace March illegal, the Police Commissioner had no legal grounds for holding Mack for reckless driving.

The Police Commissioner replied that reckless driving was the least of it, as there were now more serious charges against Mack. The owner of the cafeteria that Mack had driven into claimed that, whether Mack was guilty of driving recklessly or not, he *was* guilty of trespassing on private property, and he refused to withdraw his charges.

"He is also guilty of kicking a police officer," said the Police Commissioner, "and I refuse to withdraw my charges."

It was clear that the Police Commissioner was acting on principle. Mack was not a prisoner anyone would have kept around for the fun of it. And his disposition did not improve with confinement.

The fact that Frank the Flower did not seem to mind too much being in jail added to Mack's bad humor. Frank was now used to the place, of course, and he received many letters and postcards from his friends among the pushcart peddlers, as well as from the hundreds of Frank-the-Flower fans.

Morris the Florist wrote Frank every day and sent him fresh flowers twice a week. Maxie Hammerman sent him all the latest reports on how the war was going, and General Anna had promised him that he would be made a general, too, as soon as he got out of jail.

None of Frank's friends had told him—they didn't like to worry him—about the Mayor's threat to end the war by revoking the pushcart licenses. So Frank the Flower was under the impression that the pushcarts were still winning the war. Naturally, he did not believe anything Mack told him to the contrary.

Frank the Flower's general cheerfulness and his conviction that the pushcarts were winning were bound to be annoying to Mack. But what drove him wild was Frank the Flower's dart board.

An old lady, whom Frank had never met, but who had

read about him in the papers, had crocheted for Frank a large
pink and green dart board. Running in circles around the
bull's-eye, Frank's friend had crocheted twenty trucks, complete with tires, and she had included with the dart board a
generous supply of darts which she had fashioned from darning needles. (She had apologized for the darning needles—
"You would probably prefer pea-tacks," she had written
Frank, "but, as you know, tacks are very expensive just now."
She wrote Frank at the time of the Tacks Tax.)

Frank the Flower had hung the dart board on the side of
his cell, and each morning after he had finished reading his
mail, he would practice shooting down trucks. Frank's ambition—if he ever got back into action—was to be able to

justify his reputation as an ace shot. It embarrassed him that all his fans believed him to be a better shot than he was.

Whenever the prison guards came past Frank's cell, they would call out, "How are you doing, Frank?" And Frank the Flower would report, "Got seventeen out of twenty last time. That's one hundred and sixteen so far today."

Sometimes the guards even came into Frank's cell and had a go at the dart board themselves. Frank the Flower was popular with the guards, who preferred crackpots to criminal types, and they called his cell The Shooting Gallery.

After Mack was arrested, the guards took to calling the truck in the center of the target "The Mighty Mammoth." There was much cheering from Frank's cell every time some-one hit The Mighty Mammoth, and medals, in the form of flowers, from Frank's hatband, were given out for every bull's-eye scored. Mack could tell from the number of daisies or bachelor buttons a guard had pinned to his uniform, how many Mighty Mammoths he had hit.

When Mack heard Frank the Flower and the guards laughing and calling out their scores, he would throw his dinner plate into the corridor and demand to be given a quieter cell. At such times, one of the guards would go across the hall and tell Mack to lower his voice as he was disturbing the customers in The Shooting Gallery.

At night when there were no guards around, Mack would call threateningly across the hall to Frank. "You just wait," he'd say. "Just wait. This war is as good as over. And when it *is*—!"

But he did not succeed in worrying Frank the Flower at all. Frank took the very fact of Mack's still being in jail as a sign that things were going very well, indeed, for the pushcarts.

After a week of Frank the Flower's optimism, Mack's own confidence cracked. A guard found him one morning crouched under his bunk, writing a desperate letter to The Three, begging them to surrender.

"An old lady is supplying them with ammunition," Mack wrote, "and thousands of officers are in training, and they will not stop until every Mighty Mammoth is extinct."

The guards confiscated the letter and gave it to the Police Commissioner. The Police Commissioner laughed and said, "Mail it to Moe Mammoth. Special delivery."

CHAPTER XXXIII

The Turning Point: the War of Words

Frank the Flower's faith, unfortunately, could not be shared by any of the pushcart peddlers who knew the facts. Things had never looked worse for the peddlers. From the time the Mayor had threatened to revoke the pushcart licenses, most of them had given up hope. Even Maxie Hammerman, though he was now famous and on a magazine cover as "The Pushcart King of America" and "The Brains Behind the Pushcart Conspiracy," was very glum.

"A great kind of king to be when soon there will be no pushcarts," Maxie said privately to his friends.

"Who is giving up?" said General Anna. "So now we must fight the City Council."

"City Councils you can't fight," Maxie said somberly. "They meet in private. You don't meet them on the streets."

"Until now," Maxie explained, "the pushcarts had a lawful right to be on the streets and we could fight for our rights. But if the City Council makes a law against pushcarts, then we have no rights to fight for. If we fight, we are against the law."

The whole city seemed to accept the fact that the Pushcart War was over. A newspaper ran a story called "The Death of the Pushcarts."

However, there was to be one more battle, and it was to

the case remains wide open. Apologists for the Mayor say
"There is a complete ... he can take no action on
physical evidence, n ... matters without first c
tion of t ... ng the possible react
... instant

be provoked by a picture, the photograph Marvin Seeley had taken months before, of Mack hitting Morris the Florist the first time. Everyone was curious at this point to know just how the war had begun, and this prompted Emily Wisser to show her husband, Buddy Wisser, Marvin's Honorable Mention picture in her scrapbook.

Buddy, as we know, blew up Marvin's picture to get a clearer view of the situation, and as the facts he discovered by enlarging the picture had human interest, he decided to publish the picture on the front page of his newspaper.

Buddy Wisser was as surprised as anyone else at what happened next. Buddy thought of himself as a hard-working editor putting together a few facts. He had no idea of the chain reaction that would be set off by the Seeley picture.

For Marvin Seeley's photo touched off the most heated, and certainly the oddest, battle of the war. This battle did not take place in the streets. It took place entirely in words, and it was to prove the turning point in the war.

Overnight all the newspapers in the city began to get letters about the pushcarts. The following letters, for instance, all appeared in the June 18th edition of one of the city papers:

Dear Mr. Editor:
    If there aren't any pushcarts, where can you get peanuts in the park to feed the squirrels?
                                                    Larry Gilbert, Age 8

Dear Editor:
    I work in the garment business. I sew the sleeves in coats. I have been sewing in the sleeves for 35 years and I like my job, but I do not make so much money that I can eat my lunch in a restaurant. What I like to do is to buy a hot dog & sauerkraut, or else a hot sweet potato, from the pushcart of Harry the Hot Dog.
    Harry comes by my place of business every noon hour. From Harry the Hot Dog, you can buy for twenty cents a good lunch. For twenty-five cents, even a piece of fruit afterward. Several of my friends buy the same.
                                                    Bessie Schwartz

Dear Editor:
    My husband has a pushcart, and if they make the pushcarts get off the streets, I don't know what I will do because the only peace I get is when he is pushing the cart. I love my husband, but a man should have some work to do.
                                                    Mrs. Bertha Beneker

Dear Editor:

Every afternoon when we get out of school, we buy Good Humors from the Good Humor pushcart that stops by our school playground. If we cannot get a Good Humor after a hard day at school, we will be pretty mad.

> Sally Beck
> Harold Jayne
> Keith Amish
> Robert Williams
> Gene Smith
> Mary Wahle
> Vivien Vercrouse
> George Vogt
> Joe Maier
> Betty Rosenbauer
> Arlene Enderlin
> Bernie Schreiber
> Ballison Fulton
> Warren Heard
> Warren Neely
> Vera Burkhardt
> Eleanor Rojanski
> (*The Second Grade of P.S. 42*)

Dear Editor:

I would be grateful if you would print in your paper that I am 99 years old and cannot walk very far. A pushcart with bananas comes by my door every morning and stops outside my window if I wave my hand. I live almost entirely on bananas, and I do not know what I would do without this pushcart.

> Mrs. Clara Washington

Dear Editor:

I am in the plastic objects business, and all the plastic objects I get come packed in big cardboard cartons. After I unpack the merchandise, I have to get rid of the cartons, because I have no room in my shop for such big boxes.

A truck will charge me $10 an hour to take the boxes away, because the truckers cannot be bothered for less. But there is a man with a pushcart who will take away these cartons at no cost to me, because he gets calls from people with merchandise to pack who need the cartons I do not need. If I have to pay a truck $10 an hour, I may as well go out of business.

E. Siegel

Dear Editor:

Last week a truck smashed in the fender of a lovely little car I bought in Paris, France. The driver did it on purpose. I know just how the pushcart men feel, and I think we should do everything we can to help them.

Nancy Raeburn

Dear Editor:

I am in the 2nd-hand and junk line, and I get almost all goods I sell in my shop from the pushcart men who go around the streets picking up things that people have thrown away, but which maybe someone else could use. I would like to ask you how I can stay in business if nobody picks up old toasters and chairs and all kinds of hardware. You'd be surprised what people are throwing out. I got from a pushcart last week an egg-beater practically as good as new. In addition, the pushcarts are cleaning up the streets.

Si Biski

Dear Editor:

I am an artistic person, and I want to say that I think the pushcarts with their striped umbrellas and big old-fashioned wheels are a very pretty sight. I have painted many pictures of pushcarts. All of the trucks are ugly.

R. Solbert

Dear Editor:

Here is a fact I know will be of interest to all animal lovers. My cocker spaniel named Cookie, who has been with me for eleven years, grows very nervous whenever a big truck passes us on the street. But she loves pushcarts and will go right up to one and let the owner pet her. Now that there are so many trucks on the streets, I really dread taking Cookie for a walk.

Arthur Winkle

Dear Editor:
A year ago I retired to the island of Rubanga. There are no trucks on Rubanga. We make our own peanut butter, and I am very happy.
I am sorry to read that you are still having trouble in the city.
Archie Love

Dear Editor:
I have never written a letter to a newspaper before, but the picture of that Mighty Mammoth hitting that pushcart has upset me so much that I cannot sleep at night. The whole thing does not seem right to me.
Jean F. Merrill

Dear Editor:
Is New York being run for trucks or people? Pushcarts are pushed by people who sell goods to other people who buy from the pushcarts out of choice. Who needs 400 cartons of peanut butter?
Committee for the Preservation
of Pushcarts

Dear Editor:
Since crowded streets seem to be our trouble, wouldn't it be more helpful to get rid of 300,000 trucks than 500 pushcarts?
Committee for the Revocation
of Truck Licenses

Dear Editor:
I just hate trucks.
A Loyal Reader

Dear Editor:

I have followed with interest the concern your readers have been expressing over the plight of the pushcart peddlers in your city. It may interest your readers to know that in our city (Harmony, Illinois), we have passed a law which makes the sale, manufacture, or operation of a truck a criminal offense, punishable by a fine of $20,000 or 20 years in jail.

Elmer P. Kusse

Dear Editor:

I have read about Maxie Hammerman, the Pushcart King, in your paper. I am wondering why there isn't any Pushcart Queen. It is my ambition when I grow up to be the Pushcart Queen.

Alice Myles, Age 10

This was only the beginning. Each letter to an editor that was published seemed to inspire a hundred other people to write. Buddy Wisser said that he had never received so much mail in his entire life as an editor as suddenly came to him on the subject of pushcarts. Even though the editors could publish only a very small sampling of the letters they received, about one out of a thousand, the "Letters to the Editor" sections of the newspapers were within a week taking up so much space that several papers had to cut out their sports, news, and comic sections.

The truck drivers did not know what to make of the hundreds of letters in the newspapers. It appeared from the letters that *everyone* who was not a truck driver was on the side of the pushcarts.

Some of the truck drivers tried to laugh off the letters. "What are a few letters to the newspapers?" they asked each other. "Everyone knows only crackpots write to the papers."

Mayor Emmett P. Cudd, however, was not laughing. "Crackpots have a vote like everyone else," he told his wife, Ethel P. Cudd. "And enough crackpots could vote a mayor into office. Or out," he added.

The Three were not laughing either. When Big Moe read Elmer P. Kusse's letter about making the driving of a truck a criminal offense, Big Moe knew it was time to surrender.

It was clear to Big Moe that the people of New York were already on the side of the pushcarts. If the Mayor's threat to revoke the pushcart licenses was carried out, people would be even angrier with the trucks. The possibility of people voting the trucks off the street entirely, as Elmer P. Kusse suggested, was not a risk Big Moe was willing to take.

Louie Livergreen wanted to proceed with the Master Plan. He said that once Operation Krushkar was rolling, people would be afraid to vote against the trucks. However, Big Moe's faith in the Master Plan had not been the same since Maxie Hammerman had captured his bulletproof Italian car. And the word "extinct" in Mack's special delivery letter had sent shivers down his spine.

"How can the Master Plan be carried out," asked Big Moe, "when we are in so much trouble with the pushcarts which you guaranteed would be a pushover?"

The Tiger voted with Big Moe to come to terms with the pushcarts and on July 4th, Big Moe telephoned the Mayor, who was just about to call Big Moe.

Big Moe told the Mayor that he was willing to meet with Maxie Hammerman and work out an agreement that would be acceptable to both sides. This was exactly what the Mayor had been about to suggest and was, of course, exactly what the Peace Army had been fighting for.

"In other words," said Maxie Hammerman, looking more surprised than he had ever looked in his life, "we have won the war."

CHAPTER XXXIV

The Battle of Bleecker Street

If any of the truck drivers thought Big Moe had given in too easily to the letters to the editors, The Battle of Bleecker Street convinced them otherwise. This was a freak battle in that it took place after Big Moe's surrender, but before the Pushcart Peace Conference which spelled out the terms of the surrender.

The day after Big Moe's surrender, all the pushcarts were on the streets again. Wherever they appeared, people cheered wildly, especially down on Bleecker Street.

On Bleecker Street, between Sixth and Seventh Avenues, some dozen pushcarts lined up, end-to-end, along the north curb every day to form a kind of outdoor market. From the pushcarts on Bleecker Street, a housewife could buy anything she needed in the fresh fruit and vegetable line, without ever having to step inside a store.

On the day after Big Moe's surrender, the pushcarts that regularly did business on Bleecker Street were joined by many of their friends. For it seemed likely that the outdoor market would attract many people after all the newspaper stories about the Pushcart War.

There must have been thirty pushcarts in Bleecker Street that morning, and there was still more business than the push-carts could handle. Women crowded around the carts, ex-

claiming over the quality of the fruit and comparing bargains.

Papa Peretz, who had come down to join the fun—although fruit and vegetables were not his line—had sold out a cart of pretzels by ten o'clock and was waltzing in the street with one of the customers. At about 10:05, while everyone was cheering the waltzers, half a dozen trucks came down the street.

"Here they come!" shouted an excitable young woman. "Those dirty trucks!" And she picked a ripe cantaloupe out of a sack of cantaloupes she had just purchased and hurled it straight through the open window of one of the trucks.

The driver she hit crashed into the truck ahead of him, and the trucks behind him slammed on their brakes. Then before the pushcart peddlers realized what was happening, their customers were all grabbing cantaloupes and tomatoes and peaches from the crates on the curb where the peddlers threw any spoiled vegetables and fruits they found in unpacking their produce each morning.

"Have a peach," a lady shouted, pitching a mouldy peach at another truck.

"Have a melon," called another.

"A nice soft pear!"

"A rotten apple!"

"A little salad," said someone, tossing out a head of lettuce.

"A nice fresh fish!" The owner of a fish store along the sidewalk could not resist making a contribution and flung a fat flounder into one of the cabs.

"All the tomatoes you want!" said an old lady, generously emptying her whole shopping bag.

The truck drivers leaped from their trucks and tried to run for cover, but they were surrounded. The ladies were pelting them from all sides. A truck driver dodged an overripe mango, only to be conked by a cabbage.

The air was filled with flying fruit and vegetables—peaches, pears, apples, pomegranates, cucumbers, cabbages, and cantaloupes. Mainly cantaloupes, as this fruit had just come into season.

At 10:30, a siren sounded, and a police car screeched around the corner. Two policemen leaped from the car and seized a redheaded woman who was carefully aiming a cantaloupe.

"Hey, lady," said one of the officers, "the war's over. Haven't you heard?"

"Certainly," she said. "We're just celebrating."

"Oh," said the policeman, and looking around, he could see that everyone was laughing and in the best of spirits.

"Well, in that case," the officer said—and he took the cantaloupe from her hand and hurled it with deadly accuracy right into the back of a fleeing truck driver, knocking the fellow headlong into a cart of tomatoes.

"You're wonderful!" shouted the redheaded lady, clapping her hands and kissing the policeman. It was a wild morning.

Fifty police cars had to be dispatched to the scene before any kind of order could be restored. And then it was really only the truck drivers' finally escaping into a subway entrance that brought an end to the fighting.

The police made no arrests. The situation was clearly a case of a city celebrating the end of a long and tiring war.

It was an expensive celebration for the pushcart peddlers. In the excitement, the ladies—when they had used up the spoiled fruit and vegetables—had helped themselves to perfectly good produce from the pushcarts. Most of the ladies offered afterwards to pay the peddlers for what they had used, but many did not know which cart they had taken the fruit from. And the peddlers did not want to take their money anyway.

The pushcart peddlers were grateful for the support of the people of the city. And they told the ladies that a few melons and peaches were the least they could contribute to the celebration.

After the Battle of Bleecker Street, the truck drivers urged

Big Moe to press for a peace conference at the earliest date possible. The Mayor was glad to oblige.

It might be mentioned here that one of New York's most colorful holidays, Cantaloupe Day—or The Feast of the Cantaloupes, as it is called in Bleecker Street—is a holiday in celebration of the armistice that marked the end of the Pushcart War.

On this day, July 5th, anyone shopping in Bleecker Street is given a free cantaloupe by the fruit peddlers there. At night the street is lit up and gaily-decorated booths line the street.

One can buy Big Moe dolls and paper pushcarts and souvenir maps of the battlegrounds of the Pushcart War (replicas of Maxie Hammerman's famous battle map). There is dancing in the streets and a pea shooter contest for children. The Feast of the Cantaloupes attracts many tourists, and, indeed, no visitor to New York should miss it.

CHAPTER XXXV

*The Pushcart Peace Conference & The Formulation of
the Flower Formula for Peace*

The Pushcart Peace Conference opened on July 13th. After
the long summer of bitter fighting, representatives of both
sides met in the City Council chambers.

Big Moe and Mack represented the truckers. Maxie Hammerman and General Anna spoke for the pushcart peddlers.
Buddy Wisser and Wenda Gambling represented the general
public. Mayor Emmett P. Cudd presided over the Conference.

General Anna's terms for peace were simple: "The City Council should revoke all truck licenses."

Big Moe protested. He had come to bargain, he said. "That is not a bargain. That is total surrender."

"Why should we settle for less?" said General Anna.

Maxie Hammerman explained to Big Moe that General Anna had lost two carts in the war and naturally felt a little bitter on that account.

This led to the first two conditions of the peace: the first, that Mammoth Moving must pay for all damages to push-carts, goods, and peddlers caused by Mack's driving into the Peace Army; second, that Mack was to have his driving license revoked for a period of one year.

The third condition agreed upon had to do with the size of the trucks that should be allowed in the city. There was some difference of opinion as to how big was too big.

The majority of those present at the Peace Conference felt that trucks the size of the Mighty Mammoths (or Leaping Lemas or Ten-Ton Tigers) were "much too big." They also agreed that trucks the size of the Mama Mammoths were "perhaps bigger than they needed to be."

Wenda Gambling insisted to the end that even the Baby Mammoths were too big. Big Moe pleaded that for moving a big item like a power plant, a truck had to be "a little bit big." And it was finally agreed that a few trucks could be as big as the Baby Mammoths, but that *no* truck should be any bigger.

The fourth condition provoked the most argument. This

214

had to do with the number of trucks that should be licensed for use in the city. Even Maxie Hammerman conceded that the city needed a *few* trucks.

"I, myself, will call a truck sometimes," Maxie admitted. "The fact is that if I order a whole truckload of lumber for building pushcarts, I get a better price on the lumber than when I order a few boards at a time."

Big Moe was prepared to agree to a *few* less trucks. General Anna wanted to hold out for a *lot* less. It looked as if the Peace Conference was going to bog down on this point. It might have, if it had not been for Buddy Wisser proposing, after the argument had run on for four days, that the Conference consider a compromise based on the Flower Formula.

The Flower Formula was something Frank the Flower had worked out while shooting darts in jail. He had told Buddy Wisser about it when Buddy went to see him in connection with his study of Marvin Seeley's picture.

The formula was really very simple. So simple, in fact, that many people afterwards said, *"I could have told them that."* But as no one had, Frank the Flower is given official credit.

Every high school student in New York is now familiar with the Flower Formula. Here is the formula as it appears on page 16 of the new edition of the math book now used in all New York City schools:

$$\textit{If: } T = \text{trucks}$$
$$\textit{And: } t = \text{time}$$
$$\textit{Then: } \tfrac{1}{2} T = \tfrac{1}{2} t$$

The example given with the formula on page 16 is the same one that was originally presented to the Pushcart Peace Conference:

If: there are 100,000 trucks (100,000 T) in the city, traffic will be so bad that it will take 10 hours (10 t) to deliver a load of potatoes from 1st Street to 100th Street.

But if: there are only ½ as many trucks (50,000 T), traffic will only be ½ as bad, and it will take only ½ as long (5 t) to deliver a load of potatoes from 1st Street to 100th Street.

Therefore: one truck can make two trips in one day.

Which means: 50,000 trucks, making two trips a day, can deliver as many potatoes as 100,000 trucks making one trip.

Moreover: if the potato dealer is paying the truckers by the hour, he will be getting two loads delivered for the price of one.

Thus: he can sell the potatoes for less (which his customers will appreciate).

Result: everybody (including pushcart peddlers) will be happier.

Professor Lyman Cumberly has pointed out that the fascinating thing about the Flower Formula is that its principle can be carried even further than was proposed at the Pushcart Peace Conference. For example, says Professor Cumberly:

If: there are only ¼ as many trucks, traffic will be only
¼ as bad (that is to say, 4 times faster), and you
will get 4 loads of potatoes for the price of one.

Or: if there are only 1/10 as many trucks, traffic will be
10 times as fast, etc;

Or: if there are only 1/100 as many trucks, traffic will
be 100 times as fast, etc.

One could, in fact, Professor Cumberly says jokingly, keep on reducing the number of trucks almost indefinitely without hurting business at all.

It is unlikely, however, that Big Moe would have agreed at the Peace Conference to so drastic a reduction of trucks as Professor Cumberly has visualized. He did agree to the one-half formula, and as Maxie Hammerman pointed out, the fact that the one-half remaining trucks would be approximately one-half as big as most of the trucks had been before the war meant that the pushcarts had won the equivalent of an agreement to four times fewer trucks.

There was an additional condition in the peace treaty. This fifth condition was an amnesty clause; it provided that Frank the Flower, in view of his contribution to the fourth condition of the treaty, should be excused from serving the balance of the sentence he would normally be expected to serve for the willful destruction of 18,991 truck tires.

The final act of the Peace Conference was to draw up the

Courtesy Act (which the City Council passed by a unanimous vote the following week). The Courtesy Act made it a criminal offense for a larger vehicle to take advantage of a smaller vehicle in any way.

CHAPTER XXXVI

The Post-War Years: A Few Last Words About Albert P. Mack, Wenda Gambling, Joey Kafflis, General Anna, Harry the Hot Dog, Mayor Emmett P. Cudd, Frank the Flower, Louie Livergreen, and Alice Myles, the Pushcart Queen

In the ten years since the Pushcart War, the Courtesy Act has been strictly observed by most of the truck drivers in New York. There have been exceptions, of course. Albert P. Mack has been arrested nineteen times for violation of the Act and is now serving a life sentence. But, as Professor Cumberly says, that might have been predicted.

What no one would have predicted, however, was that Wenda Gambling would marry a former truck driver. She is now Mrs. Joey Kafflis. A few years ago Joey Kafflis sold his diary to a movie company that was making a movie about the Pushcart War, and by coincidence Wenda Gambling was chosen to play the part of Wenda Gambling, and in this way she met Joey Kafflis.

In the movie version of the Pushcart War, Wenda Gambling *does* fire the opening shot in the historic Pea Shooter Campaign, and she also appears in the front lines of the Peace March, right between General Anna and Morris the Florist. In the Peace March she is shown pushing a cart of secondhand shoes. A few of Wenda's admirers did not recognize her in this scene as she is wearing a shawl over her head.

In the movie it is Wenda Gambling, of course, rather than General Anna, who saves Morris the Florist's life. Although Wenda herself is seriously wounded, she manages to pull Morris to safety.

It is perhaps just as well that General Anna did not live to see the movie version of the Peace March. She died a few years after the Pushcart War at the age of eighty-one, and there is now a statue of her in Tompkins Square Park, the first statue of a pushcart peddler ever to be placed in a city park. The inscription beneath the statue reads simply: "By Hand."

Among the officials who spoke at the dedication of General Anna's statue was the Honorable Harold L. Kugelman, better known to veterans of the Pushcart War as Harry the Hot Dog. At that time, Harry had just been appointed Target Chief for the New York City Moon Exploration Bureau. (This is the department that sent the successful "Pea-Pin" Rocket to the north side of the moon last year.)

Harry was named as Target Chief for the MEB by none other than Mayor Emmett P. Cudd. For Mayor Cudd, despite his questionable role in the Pushcart War, was re-elected after the war for a third term.

In his post-war campaign, Mayor Cudd ran for re-election on a Potato Platform ("Two Potatoes for the Price of One"— a slogan that won him many more votes than his Peanut Butter Platform of the previous election). It was this campaign that earned the Mayor the nickname "Potato Head."

One of the yet unresolved mysteries of the war is the whereabouts of Louie Livergreen. Louie disappeared from his offices on Second Avenue a few days after Big Moe's surrender to the pushcarts.

Louie's secretary told the police that certain documents

(among them, the LEMA Master Plan for the Streets of New York) had disappeared from her employer's files at the same time her employer dropped from view. It is widely believed that the AST (Association of Small Truckers) had something to do with Louie's disappearance, but this has never been proved.

There was also a rumor at one point that Louie was alive and hiding out in Dallas, Texas, where he was said to be operating an earth-moving machinery business under another name. New York and Dallas police traced this rumor to the fact that there was a firm in Dallas known as LEMA (Lucky Earth-Moving Associates). However, on investigation, it appeared that the firm was run by a Mr. Jim Lucky, one of the best-liked young businessmen in Dallas. Jim Lucky sued a Houston newspaper for printing the rumor, which he claimed was damaging his business reputation, and since then other papers have been cautious about printing Livergreen stories.

And, finally, we cannot conclude this account of the Pushcart War without mentioning Alice Myles. Alice, who at the age of ten had written to the editor of a newspaper to say that her ambition was to be the Pushcart Queen, is well on her way to getting her wish.

Alice attended a very good vocational school and now has her own pushcart shop. Last year she built almost as many carts as Maxie Hammerman. Maxie says he does not mind the competition. He is about to retire and is glad that Alice will be carrying on the good work.

"That is what we fought the war for," Maxie says, "so that there should always be a few pushcarts in the city of New York."

J
FIC   Merrill, Jean.
Merrill   The pushcart war.

DATE			

BAKER & TAYLOR